Faithful Love

Christian romance fiction, Volume 3

Angela Marie Stewart

Published by B&H Publishing Group, 2024.

This is a work of fiction. Similarities to real people, places, or events are entirely coincidental.

FAITHFUL LOVE

First edition. August 23, 2024.

ISBN: 979-8227989451

Written by Angela Marie Stewart.

Table of Contents

Chapter 1: The Foundation of Faithful Love 1

Chapter 2: Love in Action: Faith Expressed 9

Chapter 3: Forgiveness in Love 18

Chapter 4: Trust: The Pillar of Faithful Love 28

Chapter 5: Love's Endurance Through Trials 38

Chapter 6: The Role of Prayer in Love..47

Chapter 7: Patience and Long-Suffering in Love............................58

Chapter 8: Sacrificial Love: A Christ-like Example 67

Chapter 9: Love's Role in Spiritual Growth 75

Chapter 10: The Covenant of Marriage: A Reflection of God's Covenant 85

Chapter 11: Hope in Love: A Future Together 94

Chapter 12: Love That Reflects God's Glory 103

Chapter 13: Overcoming Fear with Perfect Love.........................113

Chapter 14: Unity in Love: Becoming One 123

Chapter 15: Everlasting Love: A Promise for Eternity.................136

To those who believe in love's enduring power,

Who walk by faith and not by sight,

And who seek to reflect the heart of God

In every relationship they cherish.

This book is dedicated to you—

May your love be steadfast, your faith unwavering,

And may you always find the strength to love

With the fullness of God's everlasting grace.

With deepest gratitude and love,

To my family and friends,

For your unwavering support and belief in this journey.

And to the One who is the source of all true love—

May Your love continue to guide and inspire us all.

Chapter 1: The Foundation of Faithful Love

Introduction

In the tapestry of human existence, love is often celebrated as the most profound and transformative experience. It is a force that transcends boundaries, defies logic, and binds souls together in an inexplicable bond. But what is the foundation of this love? What gives it the strength to endure the storms of life, the patience to navigate the trials of relationships, and the kindness to heal wounds? The answer lies in the concept of love as rooted in faith—faith in God, faith in each other, and faith in the journey of life. This chapter delves into the essence of faithful love, drawing parallels between God's unwavering love for humanity and the foundation of a strong, faith-based romantic relationship.

The Nature of Love

Before we can understand the foundation of faithful love, we must first comprehend the nature of love itself. Love, in its truest form, is more than just a feeling; it is a commitment, a choice, and a way of life. The Apostle Paul, in his letter to the Corinthians, provides one of the most eloquent descriptions of love:

"Love is patient, love is kind. It does not envy, it does not boast, it is not proud. It does not dishonor others, it is not self-seeking, it is not easily angered, it keeps no record of wrongs. Love does not delight in evil but rejoices with the truth. It always protects, always trusts, always hopes, always perseveres." (1 Corinthians 13:4-7, NIV)

These verses encapsulate the essence of love in its purest form. They highlight the characteristics that make love not just an emotion but a divine principle that governs our relationships. Love, as described by Paul, is patient and kind; it is selfless, forgiving, and enduring. It is a love that mirrors the very nature of God.

God's Unwavering Love for Humanity

To understand the foundation of faithful love in a romantic relationship, we must first look to the source of all love: God's unwavering love for humanity. The Bible is replete with examples of God's love, which is often described as steadfast, enduring, and unconditional. God's love is not contingent upon our actions or worthiness; it is a love that is freely given, rooted in His very nature.

One of the most profound expressions of God's love is found in the sacrifice of Jesus Christ. John 3:16 (NIV) states, "For God so loved the world that he gave his one and only Son, that whoever believes in him shall not perish but have eternal life." This verse is a testament to the depth of God's love—a love that is willing to give the ultimate sacrifice for the sake of humanity.

This sacrificial love is the cornerstone of the Christian faith and serves as a model for how we are to love one another. Just as God loves us unconditionally, we are called to love others with the same selflessness and commitment.

The Parallel in Romantic Relationships

In a romantic relationship, faithful love is built on the same principles that define God's love for humanity. It is a love that is patient, kind, and selfless. It is a love that seeks to serve rather than be served, to give rather than receive. At its core, faithful love is rooted in the understanding that true love is not about what we can get from the relationship but about what we can give to it.

1 Corinthians 13:4-7 provides a blueprint for this kind of love. Let us explore these characteristics in the context of a romantic relationship.

1. Love is Patient

Patience is perhaps one of the most challenging aspects of love, yet it is also one of the most essential. In a world where instant gratification is often sought after, the ability to be patient with one another is a testament to the strength of a relationship. Patience means giving your partner the time and space to grow, to heal, and to become the person God has called them to be.

In the context of a romantic relationship, patience might look like waiting for your partner to overcome personal challenges, forgiving them when they fall short, and choosing to see the best in them even when they make mistakes. It is the understanding that love is not a race but a journey that requires endurance, understanding, and grace.

2. Love is Kind

Kindness is the expression of love through actions. It is the small gestures of care and compassion that communicate love in ways words often cannot. In a romantic relationship, kindness is demonstrated through the way partners speak to each other, the thoughtfulness they show in daily interactions, and the willingness to put the other's needs before their own.

Kindness in love is also about being gentle and understanding, especially in moments of conflict. It is choosing to respond with empathy rather than anger, to build up rather than tear down. Kindness fosters an environment where love can flourish, creating a safe space for both partners to thrive.

3. Love Does Not Envy

Envy can be a destructive force in any relationship. It breeds resentment and can lead to a breakdown in trust and communication. Faithful love, however, is not envious. It does not compare itself to others or seek to diminish the success or happiness of the other.

In a romantic relationship, this means celebrating each other's achievements and being genuinely happy for one another. It means recognizing that love is not a competition but a partnership where both individuals are invested in each other's growth and well-being.

4. Love Does Not Boast, It Is Not Proud

Pride and boasting have no place in a relationship built on faithful love. Love, in its truest form, is humble. It does not seek to elevate itself above the other or to assert dominance. Instead, it is characterized by mutual respect and the recognition that both partners are equal in the relationship.

Humility in love means being willing to admit when you are wrong, to seek forgiveness, and to put the other person's needs ahead of your own. It is the understanding that love is not about being right or having the upper hand but about building a relationship where both individuals feel valued and respected.

5. Love Does Not Dishonor Others

A relationship rooted in faithful love is one where both partners honor each other in word and deed. This means treating each other with respect, speaking kindly, and refraining from actions that would cause harm or embarrassment to the other. Honor in a relationship is about recognizing the inherent dignity and worth of the other person and committing to upholding it.

Dishonoring behaviors, such as lying, cheating, or speaking harshly, have no place in a relationship built on faithful love. Instead, love calls us to act with integrity, to be truthful, and to protect the reputation and feelings of our partner.

6. Love Is Not Self-Seeking

Selflessness is at the heart of faithful love. It is the willingness to put the needs and desires of your partner above your own. In a romantic relationship, this might mean making sacrifices for the sake of the relationship, being willing to compromise, and considering how your actions will impact the other person.

Faithful love is not about what you can get out of the relationship but about what you can give. It is a love that seeks to serve, to build up, and to support the other person in their journey. This selfless love is reflective of Christ's love for us—a love that was willing to lay down His life for the sake of others.

7. Love Is Not Easily Angered

Anger is a natural human emotion, but in the context of a relationship, it must be handled with care. Faithful love is slow to anger; it seeks to understand rather than react. It is the ability to approach conflicts with a calm and rational mind, to listen before speaking, and to seek resolution rather than revenge.

In a romantic relationship, this means being patient with your partner's flaws, choosing to respond with kindness rather than frustration, and working through disagreements in a way that builds rather than destroys. Faithful love is characterized by a commitment to maintaining peace and harmony in the relationship.

8. Love Keeps No Record of Wrongs

Forgiveness is a cornerstone of faithful love. It is the ability to let go of past hurts and to move forward in the relationship without holding grudges. Keeping a record of wrongs only serves to build walls between partners and to create an atmosphere of resentment and distrust.

In a relationship built on faithful love, forgiveness is freely given. It is the recognition that we are all imperfect and that love requires grace. This means letting go of past mistakes, choosing to see the best in each other, and committing to a future where love triumphs over bitterness.

9. Love Does Not Delight in Evil but Rejoices with the Truth

Faithful love is rooted in truth and righteousness. It does not find pleasure in wrongdoing or in the misfortunes of others. Instead, it rejoices in what is good, just, and true. In a romantic relationship, this means being honest with each other, upholding moral integrity, and celebrating the victories and blessings in each other's lives.

Rejoicing in the truth also means being transparent in the relationship, communicating openly, and building a foundation of trust. It is the understanding that love is strengthened by truth and that deception has no place in a healthy relationship.

10. Love Always Protects

Protection is a natural outflow of faithful love. It is the desire to keep the other person safe—physically, emotionally, and spiritually. In a romantic relationship, this means standing up for each other, providing a sense of security, and being a source of comfort and support.

Protection also involves guarding the relationship from external threats, such as negative influences, unhealthy behaviors, and anything that could harm the bond between partners. It is the commitment to creating an environment where love can flourish and where both individuals feel secure in the relationship.

11. Love Always Trusts

Trust is the bedrock of any relationship, and in the context of faithful love, it is paramount. Trust means believing in the other person's intentions, having confidence in their character, and knowing that they have your best interests at heart.

In a romantic relationship, trust is built over time through consistent actions, honest communication, and a commitment to integrity. It is the assurance that you can rely on each other, even in the face of challenges, and that the relationship is grounded in mutual respect and faithfulness.

12. Love Always Hopes

Hope is a powerful aspect of love. It is the belief in a positive future, the expectation that love will endure, and the confidence that the relationship will grow stronger over time. In a romantic relationship, hope is what sustains partners through difficult times, giving them the strength to persevere and the assurance that love will prevail.

Faithful love is characterized by a hopeful outlook, one that sees beyond the present challenges and envisions a future filled with joy, peace, and continued growth. This hope is rooted in faith—faith in God, faith in each other, and faith in the journey of life together.

13. Love Always Perseveres

Perseverance is the ability to endure through difficult times, to remain steadfast in the face of adversity, and to continue loving even when it is challenging. In a romantic relationship, perseverance is what keeps the relationship strong, even when the road is rough.

Faithful love is not easily swayed by circumstances. It is a love that is committed to the long haul, that chooses to stay even when it would be easier to leave. This perseverance is a reflection of God's unwavering love for us—a love that never gives up, never lets go, and never abandons us.

Building a Faith-Based Relationship

Having explored the characteristics of faithful love as outlined in 1 Corinthians 13:4-7, it is important to consider how these principles can be applied in building a faith-based romantic relationship. A relationship rooted in faith is one that is centered on God, where both partners are committed to growing in their faith and in their love for each other.

1. Centering the Relationship on God

The foundation of a faith-based relationship is God. When both partners are committed to putting God at the center of their relationship, they are building on a foundation that is unshakable. This means prioritizing spiritual growth, praying together, studying the Word of God, and seeking His guidance in all aspects of the relationship.

When God is at the center, the relationship is grounded in love, truth, and righteousness. It is a relationship that is built on the solid rock of faith, and it is one that can withstand the trials and challenges of life.

2. Cultivating Spiritual Intimacy

In addition to physical and emotional intimacy, spiritual intimacy is a crucial aspect of a faith-based relationship. Spiritual intimacy involves sharing your faith journey with your partner, encouraging each other in your walk with God, and growing together in your understanding of His will for your lives.

This can be cultivated through regular prayer, attending church together, participating in Bible studies, and having open discussions about your faith. Spiritual intimacy deepens the bond between partners and strengthens the relationship on a level that goes beyond the physical and emotional.

3. Practicing Forgiveness and Grace

As we have seen, forgiveness is a key component of faithful love. In a faith-based relationship, it is important to practice forgiveness and grace, recognizing that both partners are imperfect and that love requires patience and understanding.

When conflicts arise, it is important to approach them with a spirit of forgiveness, seeking to resolve issues in a way that honors God and builds up the relationship. This means letting go of past hurts, choosing to see the best in each other, and extending grace even when it is difficult.

4. Fostering a Spirit of Service

Faithful love is characterized by selflessness and a willingness to serve. In a faith-based relationship, both partners should seek to serve each other, putting the other's needs above their own and working together to build a relationship that reflects Christ's love.

This can be expressed in simple ways, such as acts of kindness, being attentive to each other's needs, and making sacrifices for the sake of the relationship. A spirit of service fosters a strong bond and creates an atmosphere of love, respect, and mutual support.

5. Trusting in God's Plan

Finally, a faith-based relationship is one that is grounded in trust—trust in each other and trust in God's plan for your lives. This means surrendering your relationship to God, seeking His guidance, and trusting that He is working all things together for your good.

When challenges arise, it is important to remember that God is in control and that He has a purpose for your relationship. Trusting in His plan gives you the confidence to face whatever comes your way, knowing that He is with you every step of the journey.

Conclusion

The foundation of faithful love is rooted in faith—faith in God, faith in each other, and faith in the journey of life together. As we have explored in this chapter, love is patient, kind, selfless, and enduring. It is a love that reflects God's unwavering love for us and that serves as the cornerstone of a strong, faith-based romantic relationship.

By centering your relationship on God, cultivating spiritual intimacy, practicing forgiveness and grace, fostering a spirit of service, and trusting in God's plan, you can build a relationship that is grounded in faithful love. This love will not only sustain your relationship but will also serve as a testament to the power of God's love in your lives.

Chapter 2: Love in Action: Faith Expressed

Introduction

Faith and love are two of the most profound and intertwined principles in Christian life. They are inseparable, like two sides of the same coin. While faith is the foundation upon which we build our relationship with God, love is the manifestation of that faith in our relationships with others. The Apostle James, in his epistle, provides a critical insight into the nature of faith, emphasizing that faith without works is dead (James 2:17). This declaration compels us to consider the practical outworking of our faith through love. In this chapter, we will explore how true love is demonstrated through actions, mirroring the way faith is expressed through deeds. We will reflect on the importance of showing love through kindness, service, and sacrifice, and how these actions not only validate our faith but also transform our relationships and the world around us.

The Relationship Between Faith and Love

Before delving into the practical expressions of love, it is essential to understand the intrinsic connection between faith and love. Faith, in its simplest form, is belief and trust in God. It is the assurance of things hoped for and the conviction of things not seen (Hebrews 11:1). Faith is the cornerstone of the Christian life, a gift from God that enables us to live in accordance with His will and to trust in His promises.

Love, on the other hand, is the outward expression of that faith. It is the practical demonstration of the principles we hold dear. The Apostle Paul, in his letter to the Galatians, writes that "the only thing that counts is faith expressing itself through love" (Galatians 5:6). This statement underscores the idea that faith is not merely an internal belief but must be outwardly expressed through acts of love.

In essence, faith and love are mutually reinforcing. Faith inspires love, and love, in turn, validates and strengthens faith. When we love others, we are living out our faith in a tangible way. Our actions become a testament to the truth of our faith, a reflection of the love of God that resides within us.

Love as an Action: The Call to Demonstrate Love

The concept of love as an action is deeply rooted in the teachings of Jesus. Throughout His ministry, Jesus emphasized the importance of love, not just as an emotion or a feeling, but as an active choice. He demonstrated this through His life, His teachings, and ultimately, through His sacrifice on the cross.

One of the most powerful examples of love in action is found in the parable of the Good Samaritan (Luke 10:25-37). In this story, Jesus illustrates that true love is not limited by social, racial, or religious boundaries. It is a love that is expressed through actions—through kindness, compassion, and service to those in need. The Samaritan's actions are a vivid portrayal of love in its purest form: selfless, sacrificial, and practical.

This parable serves as a reminder that love is more than just words or sentiments. It requires us to go beyond our comfort zones, to take tangible steps in helping others, and to live out our faith in real, impactful ways.

Love Expressed Through Kindness

Kindness is one of the most visible and accessible forms of love in action. It is the simple yet profound act of showing care, consideration, and compassion to others. Kindness, as an expression of love, is not confined to grand gestures or significant sacrifices; it is often found in the small, everyday acts that we perform for those around us.

In the Christian context, kindness is a reflection of God's love for us. The Bible is filled with references to God's kindness, from His patience with the Israelites to His ultimate act of kindness in sending His Son, Jesus Christ, to redeem humanity. We are called to emulate this kindness in our relationships with others.

1. The Power of Small Acts of Kindness

Small acts of kindness can have a profound impact on those around us. A kind word, a helping hand, or a simple gesture of appreciation can brighten someone's day and remind them of their worth. These acts, though seemingly insignificant, are powerful expressions of love.

Consider the story of Dorcas (also known as Tabitha) in Acts 9:36-42. Dorcas was known for her acts of kindness and charity, particularly in making clothes for the poor. Her deeds were so impactful that when she died, the community mourned her deeply, and her resurrection by Peter became a testament to the power of a life lived in service to others.

Dorcas's story illustrates that acts of kindness, no matter how small, are significant in the eyes of God. They are a demonstration of love that can leave a lasting legacy, touching the lives of those around us in profound ways.

2. The Challenge of Showing Kindness in Difficult Situations

While it is easy to be kind when everything is going well, the true test of love is our ability to show kindness in difficult situations—when we are hurt, frustrated, or dealing with challenging people. Jesus calls us to a higher standard of love, one that extends even to our enemies.

In Matthew 5:44, Jesus teaches, "But I tell you, love your enemies and pray for those who persecute you." This command challenges us to rise above our natural inclinations and to respond to negativity with kindness. It is a radical form of love that reflects the character of God, who is kind to the ungrateful and the wicked (Luke 6:35).

Showing kindness in difficult situations requires us to draw on the strength of our faith. It is a conscious decision to act in love, even when it is not easy or convenient. This kind of love not only transforms our relationships but also serves as a powerful witness to the love of Christ in our lives.

3. The Ripple Effect of Kindness

Kindness has a ripple effect. One act of kindness can inspire others to do the same, creating a chain reaction of love and compassion. This ripple effect can extend far beyond what we can see, impacting lives in ways we may never know.

In the book of Ruth, we see how acts of kindness can create a ripple effect. Ruth's kindness and loyalty to her mother-in-law, Naomi, set off a chain of events that ultimately led to her marriage to Boaz and her inclusion in the lineage of Jesus Christ. This story reminds us that our acts of kindness, though seemingly small, can have far-reaching consequences.

As Christians, we are called to be agents of kindness in a world that often lacks compassion. By showing kindness to others, we reflect the love of God and contribute to the building of His kingdom on earth.

Love Expressed Through Service

Service is another powerful way to express love in action. It is the act of putting others' needs before our own, of using our time, talents, and resources to help those around us. Service is a hallmark of the Christian faith, exemplified by Jesus Himself, who came "not to be served, but to serve" (Matthew 20:28).

Service is not just a duty or obligation; it is an expression of love that flows from a heart transformed by faith. When we serve others, we are living out the love of Christ in practical ways, making a tangible difference in their lives.

1. The Example of Jesus

Jesus is the ultimate example of love expressed through service. Throughout His ministry, He consistently put the needs of others before His own, healing the sick, feeding the hungry, and offering hope to the downtrodden. His service culminated in the ultimate act of love—His sacrificial death on the cross.

In John 13:1-17, we see a powerful example of Jesus' love in action through the washing of His disciples' feet. This act of service was a profound demonstration of humility and love, as washing feet was a task typically reserved for the lowest servants. By performing this act, Jesus taught His disciples that true greatness in the kingdom of God is found in serving others.

Jesus' example challenges us to adopt a posture of humility and service in our own lives. It reminds us that love is not about seeking power or recognition but about lowering ourselves to lift others up.

2. Serving Others as an Expression of Love

Serving others is a practical expression of love. It is a way of putting our faith into action and demonstrating the love of Christ to those around us. Service can take many forms, from volunteering at a local charity to helping a neighbor in need, to simply being there for a friend who is going through a difficult time.

In Galatians 5:13, Paul encourages believers to "serve one another humbly in love." This command highlights the importance of service as a key aspect of the Christian life. It is through serving others that we fulfill the law of Christ, which is the law of love.

When we serve others, we are not only meeting their physical needs but also ministering to their emotional and spiritual needs. Service is a way of showing people that they are loved, valued, and not alone. It is a way of bringing the love of God into their lives in a tangible and meaningful way.

3. The Joy of Serving

While service often requires sacrifice, it is also a source of great joy. There is a unique fulfillment that comes from knowing that you have made a positive impact in someone's life. Jesus Himself experienced this joy, as He found fulfillment in doing the will of His Father and serving others.

In Acts 20:35, Paul quotes Jesus as saying, "It is more blessed to give than to receive." This statement captures the essence of the joy that comes from serving others. When we give of ourselves—our time, our talents, our resources—we experience a deeper sense of purpose and fulfillment.

The joy of serving is not dependent on the recognition or appreciation of others. It comes from knowing that we are living out our faith in a way that pleases God and reflects His love to the world. As we serve others, we draw closer to God and grow in our understanding of His love for us.

Love Expressed Through Sacrifice

Sacrifice is perhaps the most profound expression of love. It is the willingness to give up something valuable for the sake of another. Sacrificial love is at the heart of the Christian faith, exemplified by Jesus' sacrifice on the cross. This ultimate act of love serves as a model for how we are called to love others.

1. The Sacrifice of Jesus

The sacrifice of Jesus is the ultimate demonstration of love in action. In John 15:13, Jesus says, "Greater love has no one than this: to lay down one's life for one's friends." This statement encapsulates the essence of sacrificial love—love that is willing to give everything for the sake of others.

Jesus' sacrifice on the cross was the culmination of a life lived in service to others. It was the ultimate act of love, as He took upon Himself the sins of the world and offered Himself as a ransom for many. This sacrifice was not just a physical act but a spiritual one, as Jesus bore the weight of humanity's sins and reconciled us to God.

The sacrificial love of Jesus is the foundation of our faith. It is the love that redeems, restores, and transforms us. As followers of Christ, we are called to embody this sacrificial love in our own lives, to lay down our lives for others in ways that reflect the love of Christ.

2. Sacrifice in Relationships

Sacrificial love is not limited to grand, heroic acts. It is often found in the everyday choices we make in our relationships with others. Sacrifice in relationships involves putting the needs and desires of others before our own, being willing to give up our time, resources, or comfort for the sake of those we love.

In marriage, for example, sacrificial love is essential to building a strong and lasting relationship. It means prioritizing your spouse's needs, being willing to compromise, and making sacrifices for the good of the relationship. This kind of love reflects the love of Christ for the church, as described in Ephesians 5:25, where husbands are called to love their wives "just as Christ loved the church and gave himself up for her."

Sacrificial love is also important in friendships, family relationships, and even in our interactions with strangers. It is the willingness to go the extra mile, to give without expecting anything in return, and to serve others selflessly. This kind of love requires us to step outside of our comfort zones and to put others' needs before our own.

3. The Cost of Sacrifice

Sacrifice often comes with a cost. It may require us to give up something we value, whether it be our time, our resources, or our own desires. However, the cost of sacrifice is outweighed by the blessings that come from living a life of love.

In Luke 9:23, Jesus calls His followers to take up their cross daily and follow Him. This call to discipleship is a call to sacrificial love, to a life of self-denial and service to others. It is a call to prioritize the kingdom of God above our own interests and to live in a way that reflects the sacrificial love of Christ.

The cost of sacrifice may be high, but the rewards are eternal. When we live a life of sacrificial love, we experience the joy of knowing that we are fulfilling God's will and making a difference in the lives of others. We also draw closer to God, as we learn to trust Him more fully and to rely on His strength in times of difficulty.

Faith Without Works Is Dead: The Call to Live Out Our Faith

The message of James 2:17 is clear: faith without works is dead. This statement challenges us to examine the authenticity of our faith and to consider how it is being expressed in our lives. True faith is not just a belief in God; it is a faith that is lived out through love, through actions that reflect the love of Christ.

In the parable of the sheep and the goats (Matthew 25:31-46), Jesus emphasizes the importance of living out our faith through acts of love and service. The sheep, who are welcomed into the kingdom, are those who fed the hungry, gave drink to the thirsty, welcomed strangers, clothed the naked, and visited the sick and imprisoned. Their actions were a demonstration of their faith, a reflection of their love for God and for others.

This parable serves as a sobering reminder that our faith must be more than just words. It must be evidenced by the way we live our lives, by the love we show to others, and by the actions we take to meet the needs of those around us.

1. Faith Expressed Through Works

Works are not the means of our salvation, but they are the evidence of a living faith. When our faith is genuine, it will naturally produce good works. These works are not done out of obligation or a desire for recognition, but out of love for God and for others.

In Ephesians 2:8-10, Paul writes, "For it is by grace you have been saved, through faith—and this is not from yourselves, it is the gift of God—not by works, so that no one can boast. For we are God's handiwork, created in Christ Jesus to do good works, which God prepared in advance for us to do."

This passage highlights the relationship between faith and works. We are saved by grace through faith, but we are also created to do good works. These works are the natural outflow of our faith, the tangible expression of the love of God in our lives.

2. The Impact of Faith in Action

When we live out our faith through acts of love, we have the power to make a significant impact on the world around us. Our actions can bring hope to the hopeless, healing to the broken, and light to those in darkness. They can also serve as a powerful witness to the love of Christ, drawing others to Him.

In Matthew 5:14-16, Jesus calls His followers to be the light of the world, to let their light shine before others so that they may see their good deeds and glorify the Father in heaven. This call to be a light is a call to live out our faith in tangible ways, to be a beacon of love and hope in a world that desperately needs it.

When we live out our faith through acts of love, we fulfill the Great Commission, making disciples of all nations and teaching them to obey everything that Jesus commanded (Matthew 28:19-20). Our actions become a testimony to the truth of the gospel, a reflection of the love of God that has been poured out in our hearts.

3. The Role of the Church in Living Out Faith

The church plays a crucial role in helping believers live out their faith through acts of love. It is within the community of believers that we find encouragement, support, and accountability. The church provides opportunities for service, outreach, and ministry, allowing us to put our faith into action in meaningful ways.

In Acts 2:42-47, we see a picture of the early church living out their faith through acts of love. They devoted themselves to the apostles' teaching, to fellowship, to the breaking of bread, and to prayer. They also shared their possessions, cared for the needy, and enjoyed the favor of all the people. As a result, the Lord added to their number daily those who were being saved.

This example of the early church serves as a model for how we are to live out our faith in community. The church is not just a place to hear the Word of God; it is a place to live it out, to be the hands and feet of Christ in the world.

Conclusion

Love in action is the natural outflow of a living faith. It is the practical expression of the love of God in our lives, demonstrated through kindness, service, and sacrifice. As we live out our faith through acts of love, we fulfill the command of Jesus to love one another as He has loved us (John 13:34).

The call to live out our faith through love is not just a suggestion; it is a mandate. It is a call to move beyond words and into action, to be the hands and feet of Christ in a world that desperately needs to experience His love.

As we go forth, let us remember the words of James: "Faith by itself, if it does not have works, is dead" (James 2:17). Let us commit to living out our faith through love, knowing that our actions have the power to transform lives, to bring hope to the hopeless, and to reflect the love of God to the world. In doing so, we fulfill the greatest commandment—to love the Lord our God with all our heart, soul, mind, and strength, and to love our neighbor as ourselves (Mark 12:30-31).

Chapter 3: Forgiveness in Love

Introduction

Forgiveness is the bedrock of any enduring relationship. It is the vital force that enables love to survive and thrive in the face of human imperfection. In our interactions with those we love, misunderstandings, offenses, and hurtful words are inevitable. Yet, it is through forgiveness that we can mend the fractures in our relationships, allowing love to continue growing stronger and deeper. The Apostle Paul, in his letter to the Ephesians, captures the essence of forgiveness with a powerful exhortation: "Be kind to one another, tenderhearted, forgiving one another, as God in Christ forgave you" (Ephesians 4:32). This chapter delves into the role of forgiveness in sustaining faithful love, exploring the profound connection between mercy, grace, and the healing power of forgiveness.

The Nature of Forgiveness

Forgiveness, in its truest form, is a divine act. It is the release of resentment, the letting go of past offenses, and the choice to move forward without holding onto bitterness or a desire for revenge. Forgiveness is not about excusing wrong behavior or pretending that pain does not exist; rather, it is about choosing to free oneself from the bondage of anger and allowing love to heal the wounds inflicted by others.

At its core, forgiveness is an act of mercy and grace. Mercy, in this context, is the withholding of deserved punishment or judgment, while grace is the unmerited favor and kindness extended to someone despite their wrongdoing. These two concepts are foundational to the Christian understanding of forgiveness, reflecting the nature of God's love for humanity.

In the Old Testament, the Hebrew word for forgiveness is "salach," which implies pardon or release. It conveys the idea of setting someone free from the consequences of their actions, often at a personal cost to the one offering forgiveness. In the New Testament, the Greek word "aphesis" is commonly used for forgiveness, meaning to release or send away. This word captures the essence of forgiveness as a conscious decision to release the offender from the debt they owe, symbolizing a fresh start or a clean slate.

Forgiveness is not merely a feeling but a deliberate choice. It requires humility, selflessness, and a deep understanding of the grace that has been extended to us by God. When we forgive, we mirror the character of God, who is "merciful and gracious, slow to anger and abounding in steadfast love and faithfulness" (Exodus 34:6).

Forgiveness in the Context of Faithful Love

In the context of a romantic relationship, forgiveness is essential for sustaining love over the long term. Every relationship, no matter how strong or loving, will face moments of conflict, hurt, and disappointment. These moments are inevitable because we are all imperfect beings prone to making mistakes. However, it is not the absence of conflict that defines a healthy relationship, but rather the ability to forgive and move forward together.

Forgiveness in a relationship is not just about resolving individual incidents of hurt or misunderstanding; it is about creating an atmosphere of grace and mercy where both partners feel safe, valued, and loved despite their flaws. It is a continuous process that requires both individuals to be committed to working through their differences with kindness and understanding.

Let us explore the different aspects of forgiveness in love, drawing from the theological reflection of Ephesians 4:32, which urges us to be kind, tenderhearted, and forgiving as God in Christ forgave us.

1. The Importance of Kindness and Tenderheartedness

Kindness and tenderheartedness are integral components of forgiveness. They represent the attitude and disposition with which we approach our partners when seeking to forgive or be forgiven. Kindness is the expression of love through gentleness, patience, and a willingness to understand the other person's perspective. Tenderheartedness, on the other hand, is the ability to be compassionate, empathetic, and sensitive to the feelings and needs of the other person.

In a relationship, practicing kindness and tenderheartedness creates a foundation for forgiveness. When we approach our partner with kindness, we communicate that we value them and are willing to work through the challenges that arise. Tenderheartedness allows us to connect with our partner on a deeper emotional level, understanding their pain and struggles, and offering comfort and support.

Ephesians 4:32 encourages us to be kind and tenderhearted because these qualities are reflective of Christ's love for us. Jesus demonstrated the ultimate act of kindness and tenderheartedness by sacrificing Himself for our sins, offering us forgiveness even when we did not deserve it. As we strive to embody these qualities in our relationships, we create an environment where forgiveness can flourish.

2. The Role of Mercy in Forgiveness

Mercy plays a crucial role in the process of forgiveness. To show mercy is to withhold judgment or punishment that is deserved, to extend compassion instead of condemnation. In the context of a relationship, mercy means choosing to forgive our partner even when they have hurt us deeply, even when we feel justified in holding onto our anger.

Mercy is a reflection of God's character. Throughout the Bible, we see countless examples of God's mercy toward His people, despite their repeated failures and transgressions. In the New Testament, Jesus embodies this mercy, offering forgiveness to sinners, healing the broken, and showing compassion to those who were marginalized and oppressed.

In our relationships, extending mercy means choosing to see our partner through the eyes of grace, recognizing their humanity and their potential for growth and change. It means letting go of the need to punish or seek revenge, and instead, offering forgiveness as an act of love.

The story of the prodigal son (Luke 15:11-32) is a powerful illustration of mercy in action. The father, representing God, extends mercy to his wayward son, welcoming him back with open arms despite his reckless behavior. This story reminds us that forgiveness is an act of mercy that reflects the heart of God, who is always ready to forgive and restore us when we turn to Him in repentance.

3. The Role of Grace in Forgiveness

While mercy involves withholding judgment, grace is the act of giving something undeserved. In the context of forgiveness, grace is the willingness to offer love, acceptance, and reconciliation to someone who has wronged us. It is the act of extending favor and kindness, even when the other person has not earned it.

Grace is at the heart of the Christian message. It is through grace that we are saved, not by our works, but by the unmerited favor of God (Ephesians 2:8-9). This same grace is what we are called to extend to others, particularly in the context of our relationships.

In a relationship, offering grace means choosing to forgive even when the offense is significant, even when the hurt is deep. It means choosing to love our partner despite their flaws and mistakes, and to extend the same grace that we have received from God.

Grace also involves letting go of the desire for retribution or repayment. When we forgive with grace, we are not seeking to even the score or to make the other person pay for their wrongdoing. Instead, we are offering forgiveness as a gift, freely given out of love.

One of the most powerful examples of grace in the Bible is found in the story of Joseph and his brothers (Genesis 37-50). After being betrayed by his brothers and sold into slavery, Joseph rises to a position of power in Egypt. When his brothers come to him seeking help during a famine, Joseph chooses to forgive them and extend grace, providing for their needs and reconciling with them. This story demonstrates the power of grace to heal even the deepest wounds and to restore broken relationships.

4. The Process of Forgiveness

Forgiveness is not always easy, nor is it a one-time event. It is a process that requires time, effort, and a commitment to healing. The process of forgiveness involves several key steps, each of which is essential for fully releasing the hurt and moving forward in love.

- Acknowledgment of the Hurt: The first step in the process of forgiveness is acknowledging the hurt that has been caused. This involves being honest with ourselves and with our partner about the pain we are feeling. It is important to recognize that forgiveness does not mean denying or minimizing the hurt; rather, it is about facing the reality of the pain and choosing to address it.

- Confrontation and Communication: Once the hurt has been acknowledged, the next step is to confront the issue and communicate with our partner. This requires open and honest communication, where both parties have the opportunity to express their feelings and perspectives. It is important to approach this conversation with a spirit of humility and a desire for resolution, rather than blame or accusation.

- Choosing to Forgive: Forgiveness is a choice, not a feeling. After the hurt has been acknowledged and communicated, we must make the conscious decision to forgive our partner. This involves letting go of the desire for revenge or retribution and choosing to release the offense. It is important to remember that forgiveness is not dependent on the other person's actions or repentance; it is a decision we make for our own healing and well-being.

- Rebuilding Trust: Forgiveness does not automatically restore trust, especially if the offense was significant. Trust is something that must be rebuilt over time, through consistent actions and a commitment to change. Both parties must be willing to work on rebuilding trust, with the understanding that it may take time and effort.

- Moving Forward in Love: The final step in the process of forgiveness is moving forward in love. This involves choosing to let go of the past and focus on the future of the relationship. It is about creating a new foundation based on love, grace, and mercy, and committing to nurturing the relationship in a positive and healthy way.

The process of forgiveness is not always linear, and it may take time to fully work through each step. However, by committing to the process and relying on God's grace, we can experience the healing power of forgiveness and the restoration of love in our relationships.

Forgiveness as a Reflection of God's Love

Forgiveness is not just a human act; it is a reflection of God's love. Throughout the Bible, we see God's forgiveness extended to His people time and time again, despite their repeated failures and transgressions. This forgiveness is a manifestation of His love, mercy, and grace, and it serves as the model for how we are to forgive others.

In Ephesians 4:32, Paul instructs believers to forgive "as God in Christ forgave you." This command is a reminder that our forgiveness of others should be rooted in our understanding of God's forgiveness of us. When we truly grasp the depth of God's forgiveness, it becomes easier to extend that same forgiveness to others.

God's forgiveness is unconditional, complete, and transformative. It is not based on our worthiness or our ability to make amends, but on His love and grace. When we forgive others, we are called to do so in the same way, without conditions or expectations. This kind of forgiveness is not only a reflection of God's love, but it also has the power to transform our relationships and bring healing to our hearts.

1. The Parable of the Unforgiving Servant

One of the most powerful teachings on forgiveness in the Bible is found in the parable of the unforgiving servant (Matthew 18:21-35). In this parable, Jesus tells the story of a servant who owes a massive debt to his master. The master, moved by compassion, forgives the debt and sets the servant free. However, when the servant encounters a fellow servant who owes him a much smaller debt, he refuses to forgive and has the man thrown into prison. When the master learns of this, he is furious and reverses the forgiveness, punishing the unforgiving servant for his lack of mercy.

This parable serves as a stark reminder of the importance of forgiveness. It illustrates the expectation that those who have received God's forgiveness should, in turn, forgive others. The unforgiving servant's refusal to extend the same mercy he received led to his downfall, highlighting the seriousness of withholding forgiveness.

The parable also underscores the principle that forgiveness is not optional for those who follow Christ. Just as we have been forgiven by God, we are called to forgive others, recognizing that we are all recipients of His grace and mercy.

2. The Transformative Power of Forgiveness

Forgiveness has the power to transform not only our relationships but also our own hearts. When we choose to forgive, we free ourselves from the burden of anger, bitterness, and resentment. These negative emotions can be corrosive, eating away at our peace and joy. Forgiveness, on the other hand, brings healing, restoration, and a sense of inner peace.

In the story of Joseph, we see how forgiveness can transform a life marked by pain and betrayal into one of blessing and reconciliation. Despite being sold into slavery by his brothers, Joseph chose to forgive them and to see God's hand at work in his circumstances. His forgiveness not only restored his relationship with his family but also allowed him to fulfill God's purpose for his life.

Forgiveness also has the power to transform our relationships. When we choose to forgive, we break the cycle of hurt and retaliation, creating an opportunity for healing and reconciliation. Forgiveness paves the way for a renewed relationship, one that is built on a foundation of love, grace, and mercy.

3. The Role of the Holy Spirit in Forgiveness

Forgiveness is not something we can achieve on our own. It requires the work of the Holy Spirit in our hearts, enabling us to extend the same grace and mercy that we have received from God. The Holy Spirit empowers us to forgive, even when it seems impossible, by reminding us of God's love and forgiveness toward us.

In Galatians 5:22-23, Paul lists the fruit of the Spirit, which includes love, joy, peace, patience, kindness, goodness, faithfulness, gentleness, and self-control. These qualities are essential for forgiveness, as they enable us to respond to hurt with love, to seek peace, and to extend kindness and gentleness to those who have wronged us.

When we rely on the Holy Spirit, we are able to forgive in a way that reflects the heart of God. The Holy Spirit softens our hearts, helps us to see others through the eyes of grace, and gives us the strength to let go of the pain and move forward in love.

Overcoming Barriers to Forgiveness

While forgiveness is essential for sustaining love in a relationship, it is not always easy. There are often barriers that make forgiveness difficult, such as pride, fear, and unresolved pain. However, by identifying and addressing these barriers, we can overcome them and experience the freedom and healing that forgiveness brings.

1. Pride

Pride is one of the most common barriers to forgiveness. When we are hurt, our pride may lead us to hold onto anger and resentment, believing that forgiveness would make us appear weak or vulnerable. Pride can also cause us to focus on our own sense of justice, demanding that the other person make amends before we are willing to forgive.

To overcome pride, we must recognize that forgiveness is not about conceding defeat or losing face. It is about choosing to love and value the relationship more than our own ego. Forgiveness requires humility, a willingness to acknowledge our own need for grace, and a desire to reflect the love of Christ in our actions.

2. Fear

Fear is another significant barrier to forgiveness. We may fear that forgiving someone will make us vulnerable to further hurt or that it will diminish the seriousness of the offense. Fear can also cause us to worry about the potential consequences of forgiveness, such as the possibility of the other person not changing their behavior or taking advantage of our forgiveness.

To overcome fear, we must place our trust in God, knowing that He is our protector and our healer. Forgiveness is not about ignoring the potential risks, but about entrusting the outcome to God. It is about choosing to forgive because we know that God is in control and that He can bring good out of even the most painful situations.

3. Unresolved Pain

Unresolved pain can make forgiveness difficult because it keeps the wounds fresh and the hurt alive. When we have not fully processed our pain, it can be challenging to let go and forgive. The pain may continue to resurface, leading to recurring feelings of anger, bitterness, or sadness.

To overcome unresolved pain, it is important to seek healing, both emotionally and spiritually. This may involve talking to a trusted friend, counselor, or pastor, and bringing our pain before God in prayer. It is also important to allow ourselves time to grieve and to process the emotions that accompany forgiveness. Healing takes time, and it is okay to take that time to fully work through the pain before extending forgiveness.

4. Misunderstanding Forgiveness

Another barrier to forgiveness is a misunderstanding of what forgiveness truly means. Some people believe that forgiveness means condoning the behavior, forgetting the offense, or reconciling with the offender. These misconceptions can make forgiveness seem impossible or undesirable.

To overcome this barrier, it is important to understand that forgiveness does not mean excusing the behavior or pretending that the hurt never happened. Forgiveness is about releasing the offender from the debt they owe, letting go of the desire for revenge, and choosing to move forward in love. Reconciliation may or may not be a part of the process, depending on the circumstances and the willingness of both parties to work toward it.

The Freedom of Forgiveness

Forgiveness is not just a gift we give to others; it is also a gift we give to ourselves. When we forgive, we free ourselves from the burden of carrying anger, bitterness, and resentment. These negative emotions can weigh us down, rob us of our peace, and keep us trapped in the past. Forgiveness, on the other hand, brings freedom, healing, and a sense of inner peace.

In Colossians 3:13, Paul writes, "Bear with each other and forgive one another if any of you has a grievance against someone. Forgive as the Lord forgave you." This verse reminds us that forgiveness is not optional; it is a command. But it is also a gift—a gift that brings freedom to our hearts and healing to our relationships.

Forgiveness allows us to move forward in life, unencumbered by the pain of the past. It opens the door to new possibilities, new relationships, and new experiences. It allows us to fully embrace the present and to live in the freedom of God's love and grace.

Forgiveness also strengthens our relationships, creating a foundation of trust, love, and mutual respect. When we forgive, we build bridges of connection and understanding, allowing our relationships to grow deeper and more meaningful. Forgiveness paves the way for reconciliation and renewal, giving us the opportunity to rebuild and restore what has been broken.

Conclusion

Forgiveness is the key to sustaining love in any relationship. It is an act of mercy, grace, and kindness that reflects the heart of God and brings healing to our hearts and relationships. As we forgive, we experience the freedom and peace that comes from letting go of anger, bitterness, and resentment. We also create an environment where love can flourish, allowing our relationships to grow stronger and deeper over time.

Ephesians 4:32 challenges us to be kind, tenderhearted, and forgiving, just as God in Christ forgave us. This command reminds us that forgiveness is not just an act of love, but a reflection of the love we have received from God.

As we forgive others, we demonstrate the same mercy and grace that has been extended to us, allowing God's love to flow through us and into the lives of those around us.

As we journey through life, may we be quick to forgive, slow to anger, and rich in love. May we remember the words of Jesus in the Lord's Prayer: "Forgive us our debts, as we also have forgiven our debtors" (Matthew 6:12). And may we live out the command of Ephesians 4:32, being kind, tenderhearted, and forgiving, as we walk in the freedom and love of Christ.

Chapter 4: Trust: The Pillar of Faithful Love

Introduction

Trust is the cornerstone of both faith and love. It is the invisible thread that binds hearts together, creating a foundation upon which relationships can grow and flourish. Without trust, love becomes fragile, and faith wavers under the pressures of doubt and uncertainty. In the Christian walk, trust in God is paramount, and this same trust serves as the bedrock for every romantic relationship. Proverbs 3:5-6 encapsulates this truth: "Trust in the Lord with all your heart, and lean not on your own understanding; in all your ways submit to him, and he will make your paths straight." This chapter will delve into the nature of trust, its importance in sustaining both faith and love, and how trust in God enhances trust within a romantic relationship.

The Nature of Trust

Trust is a multifaceted concept that plays a crucial role in every aspect of life. At its core, trust is a firm belief in the reliability, truth, or strength of someone or something. In relationships, trust means having confidence in the other person's integrity, honesty, and commitment. It is the assurance that the other person will act in your best interest and remain loyal, even in the face of challenges.

In the Bible, trust is often synonymous with faith. To trust in God is to have unwavering confidence in His character, promises, and plans for our lives. It is the belief that God is who He says He is and that He will do what He has promised. This trust is not based on our own understanding or circumstances but on the unchanging nature of God.

Trust is also relational. It is built over time through consistent actions, honest communication, and a demonstrated commitment to the relationship. Trust requires vulnerability, as it involves placing confidence in another person, knowing that they have the power to hurt or disappoint us. However, when trust is established, it creates a sense of security and intimacy that allows the relationship to flourish.

Trust as a Cornerstone of Faith

Trust is fundamental to the Christian faith. Without trust, it is impossible to have a relationship with God, for trust is the essence of faith. Hebrews 11:6 states, "And without faith it is impossible to please God, because anyone who comes to him must believe that he exists and that he rewards those who earnestly seek him." Trust is the belief that God is who He says He is and that He is faithful to fulfill His promises.

The Bible is filled with stories of individuals who trusted in God despite overwhelming circumstances. Abraham, known as the father of faith, trusted God when He called him to leave his homeland and journey to an unknown land. He trusted God's promise that he would become the father of many nations, even when he and his wife, Sarah, were well beyond childbearing age. Abraham's trust in God was so strong that he was willing to sacrifice his only son, Isaac, believing that God could raise him from the dead (Hebrews 11:17-19).

Similarly, David, a man after God's own heart, demonstrated trust in God throughout his life. Whether facing the giant Goliath, fleeing from King Saul, or ruling as king, David's trust in God never wavered. In Psalm 23, David beautifully expresses his trust in God as his shepherd, guiding and protecting him through every valley and shadow.

These examples illustrate that trust in God is not based on circumstances but on a deep, abiding faith in His character and promises. This trust sustains believers through trials, strengthens their faith, and deepens their relationship with God.

1. Trust and Faith: Two Sides of the Same Coin

Trust and faith are intimately connected; they are two sides of the same coin. Faith is the belief in something or someone, while trust is the confidence that this belief is well-founded. In the Christian life, faith in God is the belief in His existence, His goodness, and His sovereignty. Trust, on the other hand, is the confidence that God's character and promises are true and reliable, leading to a life of obedience and surrender to His will.

In Proverbs 3:5-6, we are instructed to trust in the Lord with all our heart and not to lean on our own understanding. This passage highlights the importance of trust as a response to faith. Faith in God leads us to trust Him with every aspect of our lives, even when we do not fully understand His ways. Trusting in God means relinquishing control, letting go of our need to understand, and allowing Him to guide our paths.

Trust is also a response to God's faithfulness. Throughout the Bible, God is described as faithful and trustworthy. In Lamentations 3:22-23, we read, "Because of the Lord's great love we are not consumed, for his compassions never fail. They are new every morning; great is your faithfulness." Trust in God is built on the foundation of His faithfulness—His unchanging nature, His steadfast love, and His unwavering commitment to His people.

2. The Role of Trust in Strengthening Faith

Trust is essential for strengthening faith. As we trust God in small things, our faith grows, enabling us to trust Him in more significant challenges. Trusting God with the details of our lives—our relationships, our finances, our future—builds a deep and resilient faith that can withstand the storms of life.

When we trust God, we acknowledge His sovereignty and wisdom, recognizing that His plans are higher than our own (Isaiah 55:8-9). This trust leads to surrender, where we relinquish our desires and expectations and place our lives in God's hands. Trust also brings peace, as we rest in the knowledge that God is in control and that He is working all things together for our good (Romans 8:28).

Trust in God also strengthens our faith by providing a foundation of stability in an uncertain world. When the circumstances of life shake our faith, trust anchors us in the unchanging character of God. It reminds us that God is good, even when life is not, and that He is faithful to fulfill His promises, even when we cannot see the way forward.

3. Trusting God Through Trials

Trust is most powerfully demonstrated in times of trial. It is easy to trust God when life is going well, but true trust is revealed when we face difficulties and uncertainties. Trials test our faith and challenge our trust in God, but they also provide an opportunity for growth and deeper intimacy with Him.

The story of Job is a profound example of trust in the midst of suffering. Job was a righteous man who lost everything—his wealth, his health, and his family—yet he continued to trust in God. In Job 13:15, he declares, "Though he slay me, yet will I hope in him." Job's trust in God was not based on his circumstances but on his deep faith in God's goodness and sovereignty.

Trusting God through trials requires us to hold onto His promises and to believe that He is with us, even in the darkest moments. It means trusting that He has a purpose for our pain and that He will bring good out of our suffering (Romans 5:3-5). Trusting God in trials also involves surrendering our need for answers and choosing to trust His character, even when we do not understand His ways.

As we trust God through trials, our faith is refined, and our relationship with Him is strengthened. We experience His presence in new and deeper ways, and we grow in our understanding of His love and faithfulness.

Trust as a Cornerstone of Love

Just as trust is foundational to faith, it is also essential for love, particularly in romantic relationships. Trust is the glue that holds a relationship together, creating a sense of security, intimacy, and mutual respect. Without trust, love becomes fragile, easily broken by doubt, suspicion, and fear.

In a romantic relationship, trust is built over time through consistent actions, honest communication, and a demonstrated commitment to the relationship. It requires both partners to be trustworthy, to act with integrity, and to prioritize the well-being of the relationship above their own interests.

Trust in a relationship also involves vulnerability. It requires both partners to open their hearts, share their fears and dreams, and place their confidence in each other. This vulnerability is a risk, as it exposes the heart to potential hurt and disappointment. However, when trust is present, it creates a safe space where both partners can be themselves, knowing that they are loved and accepted as they are.

1. Building Trust in a Relationship

Building trust in a relationship is a gradual process that requires time, effort, and intentionality. Trust is not something that can be forced or demanded; it must be earned through consistent actions and demonstrated commitment.

- Honesty and Transparency: Honesty is the foundation of trust. In a relationship, both partners must be committed to speaking the truth, even when it is difficult or uncomfortable. Transparency involves being open and honest about one's thoughts, feelings, and actions, and not hiding anything that could damage the relationship. When both partners are honest and transparent, trust is strengthened, and the relationship becomes more resilient.

- Consistency and Reliability: Trust is built through consistent actions over time. When both partners are reliable, keeping their promises and following through on their commitments, trust grows. Consistency also involves being dependable in both small and significant ways, showing up for each other and being there when it matters most.

- Respect and Consideration: Trust is also built on mutual respect and consideration. Both partners must value each other's feelings, opinions, and boundaries, and be willing to prioritize the well-being of the relationship. When respect is present, trust flourishes, creating an environment where both partners feel safe and valued.

- Vulnerability and Emotional Intimacy: Trust requires vulnerability, the willingness to open one's heart and share deeply with the other person. Emotional intimacy is built when both partners are

willing to be vulnerable, to share their fears, dreams, and insecurities, and to support each other through the ups and downs of life. This vulnerability creates a deeper connection and strengthens trust in the relationship.

- Forgiveness and Grace: Trust is not about perfection; it is about grace. Both partners will make mistakes, and trust will inevitably be tested. When this happens, it is essential to extend forgiveness and grace, to work through the issues together, and to rebuild trust through honest communication and a commitment to change.

2. The Impact of Trust on Love

Trust has a profound impact on love in a relationship. When trust is present, love is able to flourish, growing deeper and more resilient over time. Trust creates a sense of security, allowing both partners to fully invest in the relationship without fear of betrayal or disappointment.

Trust also fosters intimacy, both emotional and physical. When both partners trust each other, they are able to be vulnerable, to share their deepest fears and desires, and to connect on a deeper level. This intimacy strengthens the bond between them and creates a foundation for a lasting and fulfilling relationship.

Trust also enhances communication in a relationship. When both partners trust each other, they are more likely to communicate openly and honestly, to listen to each other's perspectives, and to work through conflicts in a constructive way. This open communication prevents misunderstandings and builds a stronger, more resilient relationship.

Trust also creates a sense of stability in the relationship. When both partners trust each other, they are able to navigate the challenges of life together, knowing that they can rely on each other. This stability provides a sense of security and peace, allowing both partners to focus on growing and nurturing their relationship.

3. Rebuilding Trust After It Has Been Broken

While trust is essential for a healthy relationship, it is also fragile and can be easily broken. Whether through dishonesty, betrayal, or neglect, trust can be damaged, leading to feelings of hurt, anger, and resentment. However, it is possible to rebuild trust, though it requires time, effort, and a commitment to change.

- Acknowledgment and Accountability: The first step in rebuilding trust is acknowledging the breach of trust and taking accountability for one's actions. This involves being honest about what happened, taking responsibility for the hurt caused, and expressing genuine remorse. Without acknowledgment and accountability, it is impossible to begin the process of rebuilding trust.

- Open and Honest Communication: Rebuilding trust requires open and honest communication. Both partners must be willing to talk about what happened, to express their feelings and needs, and to listen to each other's perspectives. This communication should be done in a spirit of humility and a desire to understand and heal the relationship.

- Commitment to Change: Trust can only be rebuilt if there is a genuine commitment to change. This involves making the necessary changes to prevent the breach of trust from happening again, whether it be through improved communication, setting boundaries, or addressing underlying issues. Both partners must be committed to working together to rebuild trust and to create a stronger, healthier relationship.

- Patience and Time: Rebuilding trust takes time and patience. It is a gradual process that cannot be rushed. Both partners must be willing to give each other time to heal, to rebuild confidence, and to restore the relationship. Trust is rebuilt through consistent actions over time, demonstrating that the commitment to change is genuine and lasting.

- Forgiveness and Grace: Finally, rebuilding trust requires forgiveness and grace. Both partners must be willing to let go of the past, to forgive each other for the hurt caused, and to extend grace as they work together to rebuild the relationship. Forgiveness is essential for healing, and grace is necessary for moving forward.

Trust in God: The Foundation for Trust in a Relationship

Trust in God is the foundation for trust in a relationship. When both partners have a deep trust in God, they are able to trust each other more fully, knowing that their relationship is grounded in His love and guidance. Trusting in God strengthens the relationship, providing a foundation of faith, hope, and love.

1. Trusting God with the Relationship

Trusting God with the relationship means placing the relationship in His hands, seeking His guidance, and relying on His wisdom. It involves surrendering the relationship to God, trusting that He has a plan and purpose for it, and seeking His will in all things.

When both partners trust God with the relationship, they are able to navigate the challenges of life with confidence, knowing that God is in control. They are able to make decisions together, seeking God's guidance and wisdom, and trusting that He will lead them in the right direction.

Trusting God with the relationship also means relying on His strength and grace to overcome challenges. When difficulties arise, both partners can turn to God in prayer, seeking His help and guidance, and trusting that He will provide the strength and wisdom needed to overcome the challenges together.

2. Trusting God to Meet Each Other's Needs

Trusting God in a relationship also involves trusting Him to meet each other's needs. In a healthy relationship, both partners seek to meet each other's emotional, physical, and spiritual needs. However, there are times when one partner may fall short, or when the needs are too great for the other to meet.

Trusting God to meet each other's needs involves recognizing that God is the ultimate source of love, comfort, and strength. It means turning to God in prayer, seeking His help in meeting each other's needs, and trusting that He will provide the grace and strength needed to love and support each other.

Trusting God to meet each other's needs also involves recognizing that He is the one who ultimately satisfies the deepest longings of the heart. While it is important for both partners to love and support each other, they must also recognize that only God can truly fulfill the deepest desires of the soul. By trusting God to meet each other's needs, both partners are able to find fulfillment and satisfaction in Him, allowing their love for each other to grow and flourish.

3. Trusting God in Times of Uncertainty

Trusting God in times of uncertainty is essential for maintaining trust in a relationship. Life is full of uncertainties, and relationships are no exception. There will be times when the future is unclear, when challenges arise, and when doubts and fears creep in.

In these times of uncertainty, both partners must trust God to guide and sustain them. Trusting God in uncertainty means surrendering control, letting go of the need to have all the answers, and trusting that God is in control. It involves turning to God in prayer, seeking His wisdom and guidance, and trusting that He will provide the strength and grace needed to navigate the challenges together.

Trusting God in uncertainty also involves trusting that He has a plan and purpose for the relationship. It means believing that God is at work, even in the midst of difficulties, and that He will bring good out of every situation. By trusting God in times of uncertainty, both partners are able to find peace and security in His love, allowing their trust in each other to remain strong.

The Blessings of Trust in a Relationship

Trust is not only essential for maintaining a healthy relationship; it also brings numerous blessings. When trust is present, the relationship is able to flourish, growing deeper and more resilient over time.

1. The Blessing of Security

One of the greatest blessings of trust in a relationship is the sense of security it brings. When both partners trust each other, they feel safe and secure, knowing that they are loved and valued. This security allows both partners to fully invest in the relationship, to be vulnerable, and to grow together.

Security in a relationship also brings peace of mind. Both partners can rest in the knowledge that they can rely on each other, that they are committed to the relationship, and that they will work together to overcome any challenges that arise.

2. The Blessing of Intimacy

Trust also brings the blessing of intimacy in a relationship. When both partners trust each other, they are able to connect on a deeper level, sharing their thoughts, feelings, and dreams. This intimacy strengthens the bond between them and creates a foundation for a lasting and fulfilling relationship.

Intimacy in a relationship also brings a sense of closeness and connection. Both partners are able to be fully themselves, knowing that they are loved and accepted as they are. This closeness deepens the relationship, allowing both partners to grow in their love and commitment to each other.

3. The Blessing of Resilience

Trust also brings the blessing of resilience in a relationship. When both partners trust each other, they are able to navigate the challenges of life together, knowing that they can rely on each other. This resilience allows the relationship to withstand the storms of life, growing stronger and more resilient over time.

Resilience in a relationship also brings a sense of hope and optimism. Both partners can face the future with confidence, knowing that they will work together to overcome any challenges that arise. This hope and optimism strengthen the relationship, allowing both partners to grow and thrive together.

4. The Blessing of Growth

Finally, trust brings the blessing of growth in a relationship. When both partners trust each other, they are able to grow together, both individually and as a couple. This growth allows the relationship to deepen and mature, creating a foundation for a lasting and fulfilling relationship.

Growth in a relationship also brings a sense of purpose and fulfillment. Both partners are able to support each other in their personal and spiritual growth, helping each other to become the best versions of themselves. This growth strengthens the relationship, allowing both partners to experience the fullness of love and life together.

Conclusion

Trust is the pillar of faithful love. It is the foundation upon which relationships are built, providing the security, intimacy, and resilience needed for love to flourish. Trust in God is the foundation for trust in a relationship, strengthening the bond between partners and providing a source of hope and guidance in times of uncertainty.

As we trust in God with all our heart, and lean not on our own understanding, we are able to build relationships that are strong, resilient, and deeply rooted in love. Trust allows us to navigate the challenges of life together, to grow in intimacy and connection, and to experience the fullness of love and life together.

May we always seek to build trust in our relationships, trusting in God to guide and sustain us, and trusting in each other to love and support us. May we experience the blessings of trust in our relationships, finding security, intimacy, resilience, and growth as we walk together in love. And may we always remember the words of Proverbs 3:5-6, trusting in the Lord with all our heart, and acknowledging Him in all our ways, knowing that He will make our paths straight.

Chapter 5: Love's Endurance Through Trials

Introduction

Love is one of the most powerful forces in the human experience, yet it is also one of the most vulnerable. It can be shaken, tested, and even broken by the trials of life. However, just as gold is refined in the fire, so too is love refined and strengthened through the trials it endures. The Apostle Paul, in his letter to the Romans, speaks to this truth: "We also glory in our sufferings, because we know that suffering produces perseverance; perseverance, character; and character, hope" (Romans 5:3-4). This chapter explores how love is tested and refined through trials, drawing parallels between enduring faith and enduring love, and reflecting on the transformative power of perseverance in relationships.

The Nature of Trials

Trials are an inevitable part of life. They come in many forms—sickness, financial hardship, loss, betrayal, and the myriad of challenges that life throws our way. While we often wish to avoid trials, they serve a crucial purpose in our spiritual and emotional growth. Trials reveal our weaknesses, test our strengths, and ultimately shape us into more resilient and mature individuals.

From a theological perspective, trials are not merely random occurrences or punishments; they are opportunities for growth and refinement. The Bible repeatedly speaks of trials as a means through which God shapes and strengthens His people. In James 1:2-4, believers are encouraged to "consider it pure joy...whenever you face trials of many kinds, because you know that the testing of your faith produces perseverance. Let perseverance finish its work so that you may be mature and complete, not lacking anything."

This passage highlights the transformative power of trials. While trials can be painful and difficult, they also have the potential to bring about significant growth and maturity. This is true not only for individuals but also for relationships. Just as faith is strengthened through trials, so too is love. When love endures through trials, it becomes deeper, more resilient, and more capable of withstanding the storms of life.

The Parallel Between Faith and Love

The connection between faith and love is profound and inseparable. Both faith and love require trust, commitment, and perseverance. Just as faith is tested and refined through trials, so too is love. The endurance of faith is often a reflection of the endurance of love, as both are rooted in a deep commitment to God and to one another.

1. Faith and Love: Built on Trust

Both faith and love are built on trust. In the context of faith, trust is the belief in God's goodness, His promises, and His sovereignty. It is the confidence that God is who He says He is and that He will fulfill His promises, even when circumstances suggest otherwise.

Similarly, love is built on trust. In a relationship, trust is the belief in the other person's integrity, their commitment to the relationship, and their love. Trust is the foundation that allows love to grow and flourish, creating a sense of security and intimacy between partners.

Just as faith is tested through trials, so too is trust in a relationship. When trust is tested, love is challenged. However, when both faith and love are rooted in a deep trust in God and in one another, they have the resilience to endure even the most challenging trials.

2. Commitment: The Heart of Faith and Love

Commitment is at the heart of both faith and love. Faith requires a commitment to God, a willingness to follow Him and to trust Him, even when the path is difficult or unclear. This commitment is not based on feelings or circumstances but on a deep conviction of God's goodness and faithfulness.

Similarly, love requires a commitment to the relationship, a willingness to persevere through difficulties and to choose love, even when it is hard. This commitment is not based on fleeting emotions but on a deep, abiding love for the other person and a desire to honor the relationship.

The endurance of both faith and love is a reflection of this commitment. When trials come, commitment is what keeps both faith and love alive. It is the decision to stay the course, to trust in God's plan, and to continue loving, even when the way is difficult.

3. Perseverance: The Key to Endurance

Perseverance is the key to endurance in both faith and love. In the context of faith, perseverance is the steadfastness to continue believing, praying, and trusting God, even when faced with challenges and doubts. It is the determination to hold on to God's promises, knowing that He is faithful.

In the context of love, perseverance is the steadfastness to continue loving, forgiving, and supporting one another, even when the relationship is tested by trials. It is the determination to work through difficulties, to grow together, and to remain committed to the relationship.

Perseverance in both faith and love leads to maturity and growth. It produces character, as Paul writes in Romans 5:3-4, and this character, in turn, produces hope. When love endures through trials, it becomes stronger, more resilient, and more capable of withstanding future challenges.

How Love is Tested Through Trials

Love is tested in many ways through the trials of life. Each trial presents an opportunity for love to be refined and strengthened, but it also presents a challenge that must be faced with courage, commitment, and faith.

1. Financial Hardships

Financial hardships are one of the most common trials that test love. Whether it is the loss of a job, unexpected expenses, or long-term financial struggles, money issues can put a significant strain on a relationship. Financial stress can lead to arguments, resentment, and a breakdown in communication, all of which can weaken love.

However, financial hardships also provide an opportunity for love to be strengthened. When both partners are committed to working together, supporting one another, and making sacrifices for the good of the relationship, love can endure and even grow stronger. Financial struggles can teach partners the value of teamwork, communication, and mutual support, all of which are essential for a healthy and enduring relationship.

One of the most important ways to navigate financial hardships is through open and honest communication. Both partners must be willing to talk about their financial situation, their concerns, and their goals. This communication should be done with love and respect, avoiding blame or criticism. By working together and making decisions as a team, partners can strengthen their bond and build a more resilient relationship.

2. Health Challenges

Health challenges, whether they involve physical illness, mental health issues, or long-term disabilities, can be some of the most difficult trials a relationship will face. When one partner is struggling with their health, it can place a significant emotional, physical, and financial burden on the relationship. These challenges can lead to feelings of frustration, helplessness, and even resentment.

However, health challenges also provide an opportunity for love to be demonstrated in profound ways. When both partners are committed to supporting each other through illness, providing care, and showing compassion, love can endure and even deepen. Health challenges can teach partners the value of patience, empathy, and unconditional love.

One of the most important ways to navigate health challenges is through mutual support and understanding. Both partners must be willing to be there for each other, to provide care and comfort, and to seek help when needed. This support should be given with love and compassion, recognizing that illness can be a deeply challenging and isolating experience. By standing together and supporting each other through health challenges, partners can strengthen their bond and build a more resilient relationship.

3. Loss and Grief

Loss and grief are some of the most painful trials a relationship can face. Whether it is the loss of a loved one, the loss of a job, or the loss of a dream, grief can place a significant strain on a relationship. Grief can lead to feelings of sadness, anger, and despair, all of which can weaken love.

However, loss and grief also provide an opportunity for love to be demonstrated in profound ways. When both partners are committed to supporting each other through grief, providing comfort and understanding, and walking through the pain together, love can endure and even deepen. Grief can teach partners the value of empathy, compassion, and unconditional love.

One of the most important ways to navigate loss and grief is through mutual support and understanding. Both partners must be willing to be there for each other, to listen, to provide comfort, and to allow each other to grieve in their own way. This support should be given with love and compassion, recognizing that grief is a deeply personal and individual experience. By standing together and supporting each other through loss and grief, partners can strengthen their bond and build a more resilient relationship.

4. Betrayal and Infidelity

Betrayal and infidelity are some of the most difficult trials a relationship can face. When trust is broken, it can lead to feelings of hurt, anger, and betrayal, all of which can weaken love. Infidelity can be a deeply painful and traumatic experience, and it can be challenging to rebuild trust and restore the relationship.

However, betrayal and infidelity also provide an opportunity for love to be demonstrated in profound ways. When both partners are committed to working through the pain, seeking forgiveness, and rebuilding trust, love can endure and even deepen. Infidelity can teach partners the value of forgiveness, grace, and commitment.

One of the most important ways to navigate betrayal and infidelity is through open and honest communication. Both partners must be willing to talk about what happened, to express their feelings, and to seek understanding. This communication should be done with love and respect, avoiding blame or criticism. By working together and seeking professional help if needed, partners can rebuild trust and restore their relationship.

5. External Pressures

External pressures, such as work stress, family dynamics, or social expectations, can also test love. These pressures can lead to feelings of overwhelm, stress, and resentment, all of which can weaken love. External pressures can also create conflicts and challenges that can strain the relationship.

However, external pressures also provide an opportunity for love to be demonstrated in profound ways. When both partners are committed to supporting each other, communicating openly, and working together to navigate these pressures, love can endure and even deepen. External pressures can teach partners the value of teamwork, communication, and mutual support.

One of the most important ways to navigate external pressures is through mutual support and understanding. Both partners must be willing to be there for each other, to listen, and to provide comfort and support. This support should be given with love and compassion, recognizing that external pressures can be challenging and overwhelming. By standing together and supporting each other through external pressures, partners can strengthen their bond and build a more resilient relationship.

The Transformative Power of Perseverance

Perseverance is the key to enduring love. It is the steadfastness to continue loving, forgiving, and supporting each other, even when the relationship is tested by trials. Perseverance is not about avoiding or denying the challenges of life; it is about facing them head-on, together, and choosing to stay the course.

Perseverance in love leads to maturity and growth. Just as Paul writes in Romans 5:3-4, "suffering produces perseverance; perseverance, character; and character, hope." When love endures through trials, it becomes stronger, more resilient, and more capable of withstanding future challenges. Perseverance also deepens the bond between partners, creating a foundation of trust, respect, and mutual support.

1. Perseverance Builds Character

Perseverance in love builds character. It teaches partners the value of patience, empathy, and unconditional love. When both partners are committed to persevering through trials, they grow in their understanding of each other and of themselves. They learn to see challenges as opportunities for growth and to approach difficulties with a spirit of love and compassion.

Perseverance also builds character by teaching partners the value of commitment. When both partners are committed to staying the course, they develop a deeper sense of responsibility and accountability to each other. This commitment strengthens the relationship and creates a foundation of trust and respect.

2. Perseverance Produces Hope

Perseverance in love produces hope. It creates a sense of optimism and confidence in the relationship, knowing that both partners are committed to working through challenges and growing together. This hope is not based on fleeting emotions or circumstances but on a deep, abiding trust in each other and in the relationship.

Perseverance also produces hope by creating a sense of stability and security in the relationship. When both partners are committed to persevering through trials, they create a foundation of trust and support that allows them to face future challenges with confidence and resilience.

3. Perseverance Strengthens the Bond Between Partners

Perseverance in love strengthens the bond between partners. When both partners are committed to persevering through trials, they develop a deeper sense of connection and intimacy. They learn to rely on each other, to support each other, and to grow together. This bond creates a foundation of trust, respect, and mutual support that allows the relationship to flourish.

Perseverance also strengthens the bond between partners by creating a sense of shared purpose and commitment. When both partners are committed to staying the course, they develop a deeper sense of responsibility and accountability to each other. This commitment strengthens the relationship and creates a foundation of trust and respect.

4. Perseverance Leads to Maturity

Perseverance in love leads to maturity. It teaches partners the value of patience, empathy, and unconditional love. When both partners are committed to persevering through trials, they grow in their understanding of each other and of themselves. They learn to see challenges as opportunities for growth and to approach difficulties with a spirit of love and compassion.

Perseverance also leads to maturity by teaching partners the value of commitment. When both partners are committed to staying the course, they develop a deeper sense of responsibility and accountability to each other. This commitment strengthens the relationship and creates a foundation of trust and respect.

The Role of Faith in Enduring Love

Faith plays a crucial role in enduring love. It provides the foundation of trust, hope, and resilience that allows love to persevere through trials. Faith in God strengthens the bond between partners, providing a source of guidance, support, and strength in times of difficulty.

1. Faith Provides a Foundation of Trust

Faith in God provides a foundation of trust in a relationship. When both partners have a deep trust in God, they are able to trust each other more fully, knowing that their relationship is grounded in His love and guidance. This trust allows both partners to navigate the challenges of life with confidence, knowing that God is in control.

Faith also provides a foundation of trust by creating a sense of stability and security in the relationship. When both partners trust in God, they are able to rely on His wisdom and guidance, knowing that He has a plan and purpose for their relationship. This trust strengthens the bond between partners and creates a foundation of love, respect, and mutual support.

2. Faith Provides a Source of Hope

Faith in God provides a source of hope in a relationship. When both partners have a deep trust in God, they are able to face the challenges of life with optimism and confidence, knowing that God is with them and that He will guide them through. This hope is not based on fleeting emotions or circumstances but on a deep, abiding trust in God's love and faithfulness.

Faith also provides a source of hope by creating a sense of purpose and direction in the relationship. When both partners trust in God, they are able to seek His guidance and wisdom, knowing that He has a plan and purpose for their relationship. This hope strengthens the bond between partners and creates a foundation of love, respect, and mutual support.

3. Faith Provides a Source of Strength

Faith in God provides a source of strength in a relationship. When both partners have a deep trust in God, they are able to rely on His strength and grace to navigate the challenges of life. This strength allows both partners to persevere through trials, to support each other, and to grow together.

Faith also provides a source of strength by creating a sense of resilience and determination in the relationship. When both partners trust in God, they are able to face the challenges of life with confidence, knowing that God is with them and that He will guide them through. This strength strengthens the bond between partners and creates a foundation of love, respect, and mutual support.

4. Faith Provides a Source of Guidance

Faith in God provides a source of guidance in a relationship. When both partners have a deep trust in God, they are able to seek His wisdom and direction in all aspects of their relationship. This guidance allows both partners to navigate the challenges of life with confidence, knowing that God is with them and that He will guide them through.

Faith also provides a source of guidance by creating a sense of purpose and direction in the relationship. When both partners trust in God, they are able to seek His guidance and wisdom, knowing that He has a plan and purpose for their relationship. This guidance strengthens the bond between partners and creates a foundation of love, respect, and mutual support.

Conclusion

Love's endurance through trials is a testament to its strength, resilience, and transformative power. Just as gold is refined in the fire, so too is love refined and strengthened through the trials it endures. When love perseveres through trials, it becomes stronger, more resilient, and more capable of withstanding future challenges.

The connection between faith and love is profound and inseparable. Both faith and love require trust, commitment, and perseverance. Just as faith is tested and refined through trials, so too is love. The endurance of both faith and love is a reflection of their deep commitment to God and to one another.

As we navigate the trials of life, may we always seek to build trust, commitment, and perseverance in our relationships. May we rely on our faith in God to guide and sustain us, and may we always remember the words of Romans 5:3-4, knowing that "suffering produces perseverance; perseverance, character; and character, hope." And may we experience the fullness of love and life together, as we walk through the trials of life hand in hand, with faith, hope, and love as our guide.

Chapter 6: The Role of Prayer in Love

Introduction

Prayer is the heartbeat of a vibrant and enduring relationship. It is through prayer that couples connect with God, draw strength, and seek guidance for their lives together. In a world filled with distractions, challenges, and uncertainties, prayer provides a steadfast anchor, grounding relationships in the love and wisdom of God. The Apostle Paul, in his letter to the Philippians, offers profound counsel: "Do not be anxious about anything, but in every situation, by prayer and petition, with thanksgiving, present your requests to God" (Philippians 4:6). This chapter explores the transformative power of prayer in nurturing a relationship, connecting with God as a couple, and seeking divine guidance and strength in love.

The Nature of Prayer

Prayer is the intimate communication between humanity and God. It is not merely a religious ritual or a set of prescribed words, but a deeply personal and relational act that allows us to express our thoughts, feelings, and desires to our Creator. Prayer is an invitation to enter into God's presence, to seek His guidance, to express our gratitude, and to intercede for others. It is the means by which we cultivate a relationship with God, aligning our hearts with His will and purpose.

In the context of a relationship, prayer takes on an even deeper significance. When couples pray together, they are not only inviting God into their relationship but also fostering a spiritual connection that strengthens their bond. Prayer creates a space for vulnerability, honesty, and mutual support, allowing both partners to grow together in their faith and love for one another.

Prayer is also an act of trust. When we pray, we are acknowledging our dependence on God and our belief that He is sovereign, loving, and capable of meeting our needs. Prayer is an expression of faith, a recognition that we cannot navigate life's challenges on our own, and a humble request for God's intervention in our lives.

The Importance of Prayer in Nurturing a Relationship

Prayer plays a vital role in nurturing a relationship, providing the spiritual nourishment and strength needed to sustain love over the long term. Through prayer, couples can cultivate a deeper connection with God and with each other, fostering a relationship that is grounded in faith, trust, and love.

1. Prayer Fosters Spiritual Intimacy

One of the most profound ways that prayer nurtures a relationship is by fostering spiritual intimacy. Spiritual intimacy is the deep connection that comes from sharing one's faith journey with another person, growing together in the knowledge and love of God. It is an essential component of a healthy and enduring relationship, as it strengthens the bond between partners and provides a solid foundation for facing life's challenges together.

When couples pray together, they are engaging in a spiritual practice that deepens their connection with each other and with God. Through prayer, they share their hopes, dreams, fears, and struggles, inviting God into the most intimate aspects of their relationship. This spiritual intimacy creates a sense of unity and purpose, as both partners seek to align their lives with God's will and to grow in their love for Him and for each other.

Prayer also allows couples to support each other spiritually. By praying for one another, partners demonstrate their love and concern, lifting each other up in times of need and rejoicing together in times of blessing. This mutual support fosters a sense of closeness and trust, as both partners know that they are not facing life's challenges alone but are supported by each other and by God.

2. Prayer Strengthens Emotional Connection

Prayer also plays a crucial role in strengthening the emotional connection between partners. When couples pray together, they create a space for vulnerability, honesty, and emotional expression. Prayer allows both partners to share their deepest feelings, concerns, and desires, fostering a deeper emotional bond.

In a relationship, emotional connection is essential for building trust, intimacy, and mutual understanding. When couples pray together, they are opening their hearts to each other and to God, creating a safe and supportive environment where they can express their emotions and receive comfort and guidance.

Prayer also provides a way for couples to process their emotions together. Whether they are experiencing joy, sorrow, anger, or fear, prayer allows them to bring these emotions before God, seeking His wisdom and guidance. This shared emotional experience deepens the connection between partners, as they learn to navigate life's challenges together with faith and trust in God.

3. Prayer Encourages Open Communication

Open communication is the cornerstone of any healthy relationship. It is through communication that couples share their thoughts, feelings, and desires, resolving conflicts and building mutual understanding. Prayer plays a vital role in encouraging open communication, as it creates a space for both partners to express their needs and concerns before God and each other.

When couples pray together, they are practicing the art of communication in a spiritual context. Prayer requires honesty, vulnerability, and a willingness to listen, all of which are essential for effective communication in a relationship. By praying together, couples learn to express their thoughts and feelings openly, to listen to each other with compassion and understanding, and to seek God's guidance in their conversations.

Prayer also encourages couples to communicate about their spiritual needs and desires. In a relationship, it is important for both partners to share their spiritual goals, struggles, and aspirations. Prayer provides a space for these conversations, allowing couples to support each other in their spiritual journeys and to grow together in their faith.

4. Prayer Provides Guidance and Direction

In a world filled with uncertainty and confusion, prayer provides the guidance and direction that couples need to navigate life's challenges. When couples pray together, they are seeking God's wisdom and discernment, asking Him to lead them in the right direction and to help them make decisions that are in line with His will.

Prayer is a powerful tool for seeking divine guidance. When couples pray for direction, they are inviting God into their decision-making process, asking Him to reveal His will and to provide the clarity and insight they need. Whether they are facing major life decisions, such as marriage, career choices, or family planning, or simply seeking guidance in their daily lives, prayer allows couples to align their decisions with God's purpose and to trust in His guidance.

Prayer also provides a sense of peace and assurance, even in times of uncertainty. When couples pray for guidance, they are surrendering their concerns and anxieties to God, trusting that He will lead them on the right path. This trust in God's guidance provides a sense of security and confidence, allowing couples to move forward with faith and hope.

5. Prayer Cultivates Gratitude and Contentment

Gratitude and contentment are essential for a healthy and fulfilling relationship. When couples cultivate an attitude of gratitude, they are able to appreciate each other's strengths, to focus on the positive aspects of their relationship, and to find joy in the simple blessings of life. Prayer plays a vital role in cultivating gratitude and contentment, as it provides a space for couples to express their thanks to God and to recognize His blessings in their lives.

When couples pray together, they are encouraged to reflect on the many ways in which God has blessed their relationship. Whether it is the gift of each other's love, the support of family and friends, or the provision of daily needs, prayer allows couples to acknowledge and give thanks for the blessings they have received. This practice of gratitude fosters a sense of contentment and joy, as both partners learn to appreciate what they have and to focus on the positive aspects of their relationship.

Prayer also helps couples to cultivate contentment in times of difficulty. When faced with challenges or unmet desires, it is easy to become focused on what is lacking and to lose sight of the blessings that are present. However, prayer provides a way to shift this focus, allowing couples to express their concerns to God while also recognizing His provision and care. This practice of gratitude in the midst of difficulty fosters a sense of peace and contentment, helping couples to navigate challenges with a positive and hopeful attitude.

Connecting with God as a Couple

Connecting with God as a couple is one of the most powerful ways to strengthen a relationship. When couples come together in prayer, they are not only nurturing their relationship with each other but also deepening their connection with God. This spiritual connection provides the foundation for a healthy and enduring relationship, as it aligns the couple's hearts with God's will and purpose.

1. The Power of Praying Together

Praying together as a couple is a powerful practice that fosters spiritual intimacy, unity, and mutual support. When couples pray together, they are inviting God into their relationship, seeking His guidance, and aligning their hearts with His will. This practice creates a sense of unity and purpose, as both partners come together in faith and trust, seeking to grow in their relationship with God and with each other.

Praying together also provides a way for couples to support each other spiritually. By praying for each other's needs, concerns, and desires, couples demonstrate their love and concern, lifting each other up in times of need and rejoicing together in times of blessing. This mutual support fosters a sense of closeness and trust, as both partners know that they are not facing life's challenges alone but are supported by each other and by God.

Praying together also helps couples to grow in their faith. When couples come together in prayer, they are creating a space for spiritual growth, as they seek to deepen their understanding of God's will and to align their lives with His purpose. This practice fosters a sense of spiritual maturity, as both partners learn to trust in God's guidance, to rely on His strength, and to grow in their love for Him and for each other.

2. Creating a Shared Prayer Routine

Creating a shared prayer routine is an essential practice for couples who want to connect with God together. A shared prayer routine provides structure and consistency, allowing both partners to prioritize their spiritual connection and to cultivate a deeper relationship with God and with each other.

A shared prayer routine can take many forms, depending on the couple's preferences and schedules. Some couples may choose to

pray together in the morning, starting their day with a time of prayer and reflection. Others may prefer to pray together in the evening, ending their day with a time of gratitude and supplication. Still, others may choose to incorporate prayer into their daily routines, such as praying before meals, before bed, or during a daily walk.

Whatever form it takes, a shared prayer routine provides a way for couples to connect with God on a regular basis. It creates a space for spiritual growth, as both partners seek to deepen their relationship with God and to align their lives with His will. It also fosters a sense of unity and purpose, as both partners come together in faith and trust, seeking to grow in their relationship with each other and with God.

3. Praying for Each Other

Praying for each other is one of the most powerful ways that couples can support each other spiritually. When partners pray for each other, they are expressing their love and concern, lifting each other up before God, and seeking His guidance and provision in their lives. This practice fosters a sense of mutual support and trust, as both partners know that they are not facing life's challenges alone but are supported by each other and by God.

Praying for each other also helps couples to grow in their love and understanding of each other. By bringing their partner's needs, concerns, and desires before God, couples learn to see each other through the eyes of grace, to appreciate each other's strengths, and to support each other in their struggles. This practice fosters a deeper sense of empathy and compassion, as both partners learn to love and care for each other in a more meaningful way.

Praying for each other also helps couples to grow in their faith. When partners pray for each other, they are creating a space for spiritual growth, as they seek to deepen their understanding of God's will and to align their lives with His purpose. This practice fosters a sense of spiritual maturity, as both partners learn to trust in God's guidance, to rely on His strength, and to grow in their love for Him and for each other.

4. Seeking Divine Guidance Together

Seeking divine guidance together is an essential practice for couples who want to align their lives with God's will and purpose. When couples seek God's guidance together, they are inviting Him into their decision-making process, asking Him to reveal His will and to provide the clarity and insight they need.

Seeking divine guidance together can take many forms. Couples may choose to seek God's guidance through prayer, asking Him to reveal His will and to provide the wisdom and discernment they need. They may also seek God's guidance through the study of Scripture, seeking to understand His principles and commands and to apply them to their lives. Still, others may seek God's guidance through the counsel of trusted spiritual advisors, seeking the wisdom and insight of those who are mature in their faith.

Whatever form it takes, seeking divine guidance together provides a way for couples to align their lives with God's will and to trust in His guidance. It creates a sense of unity and purpose, as both partners seek to grow in their relationship with God and to align their lives with His purpose. It also fosters a sense of spiritual maturity, as both partners learn to trust in God's guidance, to rely on His strength, and to grow in their love for Him and for each other.

5. Praying for Your Relationship

Praying for your relationship is one of the most important ways to nurture and strengthen your love. When couples pray for their relationship, they are inviting God into their love story, asking Him to guide and bless their journey together. This practice fosters a sense of unity and purpose, as both partners seek to grow in their love for each other and to align their relationship with God's will.

Praying for your relationship can take many forms. Couples may choose to pray for their relationship during times of difficulty, asking God for strength, guidance, and healing. They may also choose to pray for their relationship during times of blessing, thanking God for His provision and care and asking for His continued guidance and blessing.

Whatever form it takes, praying for your relationship provides a way for couples to nurture their love and to align their relationship with God's will. It creates a sense of unity and purpose, as both partners seek to grow in their love for each other and to align their relationship with God's purpose. It also fosters a sense of spiritual maturity, as both partners learn to trust in God's guidance, to rely on His strength, and to grow in their love for Him and for each other.

Seeking Divine Guidance and Strength in Love

Prayer is not only a means of connecting with God; it is also a source of divine guidance and strength in love. Through prayer, couples can seek God's wisdom, direction, and power to navigate the challenges of life and to grow in their love for each other.

1. Seeking Divine Guidance in Decision-Making

One of the most important ways that couples can seek divine guidance in their relationship is through decision-making. Whether they are facing major life decisions, such as marriage, career choices, or family planning, or simply seeking guidance in their daily lives, prayer provides a way for couples to invite God into their decision-making process and to seek His will and purpose.

When couples seek divine guidance in decision-making, they are expressing their trust in God's wisdom and sovereignty. They are acknowledging that they do not have all the answers and that they need God's guidance and direction. This trust in God's guidance provides a sense of peace and assurance, as both partners know that they are not making decisions on their own but are seeking God's will and purpose.

Seeking divine guidance in decision-making also fosters a sense of unity and purpose in the relationship. When both partners are committed to seeking God's will, they are aligning their hearts and minds with His purpose, creating a sense of shared vision and direction. This unity and purpose strengthen the relationship, allowing both partners to navigate life's challenges with confidence and hope.

2. Seeking Divine Strength in Times of Difficulty

In a world filled with challenges and uncertainties, seeking divine strength in times of difficulty is essential for maintaining a healthy and enduring relationship. When couples face trials and hardships, it is easy to become overwhelmed, discouraged, and even disheartened. However, prayer provides a way for couples to seek God's strength, to rely on His power, and to find hope in His promises.

When couples seek divine strength in times of difficulty, they are expressing their dependence on God and their belief that He is sovereign, loving, and capable of meeting their needs. They are acknowledging that they cannot navigate life's challenges on their own and that they need God's strength and guidance. This trust in God's strength provides a sense of peace and assurance, as both partners know that they are not facing difficulties alone but are supported by God's power and love.

Seeking divine strength in times of difficulty also fosters a sense of resilience and determination in the relationship. When both partners are committed to relying on God's strength, they are able to face challenges with confidence and hope, knowing that God is with them and that He will guide them through. This resilience and determination strengthen the relationship, allowing both partners to grow in their love for each other and for God.

3. Seeking Divine Protection and Provision

Prayer is also a powerful way for couples to seek divine protection and provision in their relationship. In a world filled with uncertainties and dangers, it is easy to become anxious and fearful. However, prayer provides a way for couples to seek God's protection, to trust in His provision, and to find peace in His care.

When couples seek divine protection and provision, they are expressing their trust in God's sovereignty and love. They are acknowledging that they do not have control over every aspect of their lives and that they need God's protection and provision. This trust in God's care provides a sense of peace and assurance, as both partners know that they are not facing life's uncertainties alone but are supported by God's power and love.

Seeking divine protection and provision also fosters a sense of gratitude and contentment in the relationship. When both partners are committed to trusting in God's provision, they are able to focus on the blessings they have received and to find joy in the simple pleasures of life. This gratitude and contentment strengthen the relationship, allowing both partners to grow in their love for each other and for God.

The Transformative Power of Prayer in Love

Prayer has the power to transform relationships in profound and meaningful ways. Through prayer, couples can experience a deeper connection with God and with each other, fostering a relationship that is grounded in faith, trust, and love.

1. Prayer Transforms Hearts

One of the most powerful ways that prayer transforms relationships is by transforming hearts. When couples pray together, they are inviting God to work in their hearts, to soften their hearts, and to align their hearts with His will. This transformation of the heart fosters a sense of humility, empathy, and compassion, as both partners learn to love and care for each other in a more meaningful way.

Prayer also transforms hearts by fostering a sense of forgiveness and grace. In any relationship, there will be times of conflict, hurt, and disappointment. However, prayer provides a way for couples to seek God's forgiveness, to extend grace to each other, and to restore their relationship. This transformation of the heart allows both partners to move forward in love, to let go of past hurts, and to grow in their love for each other.

2. Prayer Transforms Relationships

Prayer also has the power to transform relationships by fostering a sense of unity, purpose, and spiritual intimacy. When couples pray together, they are aligning their hearts and minds with God's will, creating a sense of shared vision and direction. This unity and purpose strengthen the relationship, allowing both partners to navigate life's challenges with confidence and hope.

Prayer also transforms relationships by fostering a sense of spiritual intimacy. When couples come together in prayer, they are creating a space for spiritual growth, as they seek to deepen their relationship with God and with each other. This spiritual intimacy fosters a sense of closeness and trust, as both partners learn to rely on God's guidance, to support each other, and to grow in their love for each other and for God.

3. Prayer Transforms Lives

Finally, prayer has the power to transform lives by fostering a sense of faith, hope, and love. When couples commit to a life of prayer, they are inviting God to work in their lives, to guide their steps, and to align their lives with His will. This commitment to prayer fosters a sense of spiritual maturity, as both partners learn to trust in God's guidance, to rely on His strength, and to grow in their love for Him and for each other.

Prayer also transforms lives by fostering a sense of hope and confidence in God's promises. In a world filled with uncertainties and challenges, it is easy to become discouraged and disheartened. However, prayer provides a way for couples to find hope in God's promises, to trust in His provision, and to experience the peace and joy that comes from knowing Him.

Conclusion

The role of prayer in love cannot be overstated. It is through prayer that couples connect with God, draw strength, and seek guidance for their lives together. Prayer fosters spiritual intimacy, strengthens emotional connection, encourages open communication, and provides the guidance and direction needed to navigate life's challenges. Through prayer, couples can experience the transformative power of God's love, allowing their relationship to grow and flourish.

As we reflect on the words of Philippians 4:6, "Do not be anxious about anything, but in every situation, by prayer and petition, with thanksgiving, present your requests to God," let us be reminded of the importance of prayer in our relationships. May we always seek to connect with God through prayer, to align our lives with His will, and to grow in our love for Him and for each other. And may we experience the fullness of love and life together, as we walk in faith, trust, and love, with prayer as our guide.

Chapter 7: Patience and Long-Suffering in Love

Introduction

Patience is one of the most vital yet challenging virtues to cultivate in any relationship, especially in romantic relationships. It is often said that love is patient, and this statement holds profound truth. Patience in love is not just about waiting but about enduring, understanding, and being steadfast in the face of difficulties. It is a reflection of God's patience with humanity—His unwavering love and grace despite our shortcomings and failures. In the same way, patience in romantic relationships requires us to show love, grace, and understanding, even when it is difficult. The Apostle Paul, in his letter to the Colossians, exhorts believers to "Put on then, as God's chosen ones, holy and beloved, compassionate hearts, kindness, humility, meekness, and patience" (Colossians 3:12-13). This chapter will explore the virtue of patience in love, reflecting on how God's patience with humanity serves as a model for how we should exercise patience in our romantic relationships.

The Nature of Patience

Patience is often misunderstood as merely waiting for something to happen or for someone to change. However, true patience is much deeper. It involves enduring hardships, remaining steadfast in the face of difficulties, and showing understanding and compassion even when circumstances are challenging. Patience is an active virtue that requires strength, self-control, and a deep sense of love and commitment.

In the Bible, the Greek word for patience, "makrothumia," conveys the idea of long-suffering, endurance, and steadfastness. It is the ability to bear with others, to be slow to anger, and to show kindness and compassion even when provoked. Patience is closely related to other virtues such as humility, gentleness, and love, and it is essential for maintaining healthy and enduring relationships.

Patience is also a reflection of God's character. Throughout the Bible, we see countless examples of God's patience with humanity. Despite our repeated failures and disobedience, God remains patient, giving us time to repent, grow, and change. His patience is a testament to His love, grace, and mercy, and it serves as a model for how we should exercise patience in our relationships with others.

God's Patience with Humanity

To understand the importance of patience in love, we must first reflect on God's patience with humanity. Throughout the Bible, we see a recurring theme of God's long-suffering patience with His people. From the story of Adam and Eve to the history of Israel, God's patience is evident as He repeatedly gives humanity opportunities to repent, grow, and return to Him.

1. The Story of Adam and Eve

The story of Adam and Eve is one of the earliest examples of God's patience with humanity. Despite giving them everything they needed in the Garden of Eden, Adam and Eve disobeyed God by eating from the tree of the knowledge of good and evil. Their disobedience brought sin into the world, resulting in their expulsion from the garden and the beginning of human suffering.

However, even in their disobedience, God showed patience. He did not immediately destroy them or abandon them but provided for their needs and promised a future redemption. God's patience with Adam and Eve is a reflection of His enduring love and His desire to see humanity restored and reconciled to Him.

2. The History of Israel

The history of Israel is filled with examples of God's patience with His people. Despite choosing Israel as His chosen nation and entering into a covenant with them, the Israelites repeatedly turned away from God, worshiping idols and disobeying His commands. Yet, God remained patient, sending prophets to call them back to Him, and giving them time to repent and return to His ways.

One of the most striking examples of God's patience with Israel is found in the book of Hosea. In this prophetic book, God uses the metaphor of a marriage to describe His relationship with Israel. Despite Israel's unfaithfulness, God remains patient, continuing to love and pursue His people, even when they turn away from Him. This image of God's patient, enduring love serves as a powerful reminder of the depth of His grace and mercy.

3. The Life and Ministry of Jesus

God's patience with humanity is most fully revealed in the life and ministry of Jesus Christ. Jesus came into the world to seek and save the lost, showing patience, compassion, and love to those who were marginalized, rejected, and sinful. Throughout His ministry, Jesus demonstrated patience with His disciples, teaching them, guiding them, and correcting them, even when they were slow to understand or quick to doubt.

One of the most profound examples of Jesus' patience is found in His interactions with Peter. Despite Peter's bold declarations of loyalty, he denied Jesus three times on the night of His arrest. Yet, after His resurrection, Jesus patiently restored Peter, reaffirming His love for him and commissioning him to shepherd His flock. This act of patience and forgiveness is a powerful demonstration of Jesus' enduring love and His desire to see His followers grow and be restored.

God's patience with humanity is a reflection of His love, grace, and mercy. It is a patience that is willing to endure, to forgive, and to give us time to grow and change. As we reflect on God's patience, we are called to mirror this patience in our relationships, especially in our romantic relationships.

The Virtue of Patience in Love

Patience is essential for cultivating and maintaining a healthy and enduring romantic relationship. It is through patience that we are able to bear with one another's flaws, forgive each other's mistakes, and grow together in love and understanding. Patience allows us to navigate the challenges and difficulties of life together, creating a foundation of trust, respect, and mutual support.

1. Patience in Everyday Interactions

In a romantic relationship, patience is required in everyday interactions. From the small annoyances of daily life to the more significant challenges of living together, patience allows us to respond with love, kindness, and understanding, rather than frustration or anger.

For example, when our partner forgets to do something they promised, it is easy to become irritated or resentful. However, patience calls us to respond with understanding, recognizing that we are all imperfect and that mistakes are a natural part of life. By exercising patience, we create an environment where both partners feel valued, respected, and supported, even when they fall short.

Patience in everyday interactions also involves being slow to anger and quick to forgive. In any relationship, there will be times of disagreement, frustration, and hurt. However, patience allows us to take a step back, to calm our emotions, and to respond with love and grace. By being patient with each other, we can resolve conflicts in a healthy and constructive way, rather than allowing them to escalate into bigger issues.

2. Patience in Times of Growth and Change

Patience is also essential during times of growth and change in a relationship. Whether it is adjusting to a new phase of life, navigating a difficult season, or working through personal struggles, patience allows us to support each other through the process and to grow together as a couple.

Growth and change are inevitable in any relationship. As individuals, we are constantly evolving, learning, and adapting to new circumstances. In a romantic relationship, this means that both partners will experience times of growth and change, both individually and as a couple. Patience allows us to support each other through these times, recognizing that growth is a process that requires time, effort, and understanding.

For example, when one partner is pursuing a new career, returning to school, or working through a personal challenge, patience allows the other partner to be supportive, understanding, and encouraging. Rather than becoming frustrated with the time and energy required for these pursuits, patience allows us to see the bigger picture, to celebrate each other's growth, and to support each other in the process.

Patience in times of growth and change also involves being willing to adapt and adjust to new circumstances. In a relationship, change is inevitable, whether it is a change in living arrangements, a shift in responsibilities, or a new phase of life, such as becoming parents. Patience allows us to navigate these changes with grace, understanding, and a willingness to work together to find new rhythms and routines that support the relationship.

3. Patience in Times of Conflict and Disagreement

Conflict and disagreement are a natural part of any relationship. However, how we handle these conflicts can either strengthen or weaken the relationship.

Patience is essential in times of conflict and disagreement, as it allows us to respond with love, understanding, and a willingness to work through the issues together.

Patience in conflict involves being slow to anger and quick to listen. It requires us to take a step back, to calm our emotions, and to approach the situation with a spirit of love and understanding. Rather than reacting impulsively or harshly, patience allows us to take the time to listen to each other's perspectives, to understand each other's feelings, and to work together to find a resolution.

Patience in conflict also involves being willing to forgive and to let go of the need to be right. In any disagreement, it is easy to become focused on proving our point or winning the argument. However, patience allows us to prioritize the relationship over the need to be right, to seek reconciliation rather than victory, and to approach the conflict with a spirit of humility and grace.

By exercising patience in times of conflict and disagreement, we can strengthen our relationship, build trust and understanding, and grow together in love.

4. Patience in Times of Suffering and Hardship

Suffering and hardship are inevitable in life, and they can put a significant strain on a relationship. Whether it is the loss of a loved one, a health crisis, financial difficulties, or other challenges, patience is essential for navigating these difficult times together.

Patience in times of suffering involves being present, supportive, and compassionate with each other. It requires us to bear with each other's pain, to provide comfort and understanding, and to walk through the difficulties together. Rather than becoming overwhelmed by the challenges, patience allows us to endure, to find strength in each other, and to trust in God's provision and care.

Patience in suffering also involves being willing to wait for God's timing and to trust in His plan. In times of hardship, it is easy to become impatient, frustrated, or disheartened. However, patience allows us to trust that God is at work, even when we cannot see the outcome, and to remain steadfast in our faith and love.

By exercising patience in times of suffering and hardship, we can grow closer together as a couple, deepen our trust in God, and find hope and strength in His promises.

The Relationship Between Patience and Other Virtues

Patience is closely related to other virtues such as humility, kindness, compassion, and love. These virtues work together to create a foundation for healthy and enduring relationships.

1. Patience and Humility

Humility is the foundation of patience. It is through humility that we are able to recognize our own limitations, weaknesses, and need for growth. Humility allows us to see ourselves and others through the eyes of grace, to recognize that we are all imperfect and in need of patience and understanding.

In a relationship, humility allows us to approach each other with a spirit of love and respect, recognizing that we are both works in progress. Rather than becoming frustrated with each other's flaws or shortcomings, humility allows us to exercise patience, to support each other's growth, and to work together to build a stronger relationship.

2. Patience and Kindness

Kindness is another virtue that is closely related to patience. Kindness is the expression of love through acts of compassion, generosity, and understanding. It is through kindness that we are able to show patience in our interactions with others, responding with love and grace even when it is difficult.

In a relationship, kindness allows us to respond to each other's needs, to offer support and encouragement, and to create an environment where both partners feel valued and loved. By exercising kindness, we are able to show patience in our interactions, to bear with each other's flaws, and to build a relationship that is grounded in love and compassion.

3. Patience and Compassion

Compassion is the ability to feel empathy and understanding for the suffering of others. It is through compassion that we are able to exercise patience in times of suffering and hardship, offering comfort, support, and understanding to those who are hurting.

In a relationship, compassion allows us to be present with each other's pain, to offer a listening ear, and to provide the support and comfort that is needed. By exercising compassion, we are able to show patience in times of difficulty, to walk through the challenges together, and to build a relationship that is grounded in love and care.

4. Patience and Love

Love is the foundation of all the virtues, including patience. It is through love that we are able to exercise patience in our relationships, showing understanding, forgiveness, and grace even when it is difficult. Love allows us to prioritize the well-being of the relationship over our own desires, to seek the best for each other, and to build a relationship that is grounded in trust, respect, and mutual support.

In a relationship, love allows us to see each other through the eyes of grace, to recognize that we are both imperfect and in need of patience and understanding. By exercising love, we are able to show patience in our interactions, to bear with each other's flaws, and to build a relationship that is grounded in love and compassion.

Cultivating Patience in Love

Cultivating patience in love is a process that requires time, effort, and intentionality. It is not something that comes naturally, but rather something that must be developed and nurtured over time.

1. Practice Self-Awareness and Reflection

One of the first steps in cultivating patience in love is practicing self-awareness and reflection. This involves taking the time to reflect on our own thoughts, feelings, and behaviors, and to recognize the areas where we need to grow in patience.

Self-awareness allows us to identify the triggers that cause us to become impatient, whether it is a particular situation, behavior, or emotion. By recognizing these triggers, we can develop strategies for managing our emotions and responding with patience and understanding.

Reflection also involves taking the time to consider our own motivations and intentions in the relationship. Are we seeking to build a relationship that is grounded in love, trust, and mutual support, or are we focused on our own desires and needs? By reflecting on our intentions, we can cultivate a mindset of love and patience, seeking to prioritize the well-being of the relationship over our own desires.

2. Practice Mindfulness and Patience in the Moment

Cultivating patience in love also involves practicing mindfulness and patience in the moment. This involves being present with our thoughts, feelings, and emotions, and responding with patience and understanding, rather than reacting impulsively or harshly.

Mindfulness allows us to take a step back, to calm our emotions, and to respond with love and grace. By practicing mindfulness, we can develop the habit of responding with patience in our interactions with others, creating an environment where both partners feel valued, respected, and supported.

Patience in the moment also involves being willing to let go of the need for immediate results or resolution. In a relationship, there will be times when things do not go as planned, when challenges arise, or when conflicts need time to be resolved. By practicing patience, we can learn to wait for the right time, to trust in the process, and to allow the relationship to grow and develop at its own pace.

3. Cultivate a Spirit of Gratitude and Contentment

Gratitude and contentment are essential for cultivating patience in love. When we focus on the blessings we have received, on the positive aspects of our relationship, and on the ways in which God has provided for us, we can develop a spirit of gratitude and contentment that allows us to respond with patience and understanding.

Gratitude allows us to see the good in our relationship, to appreciate each other's strengths, and to focus on the positive aspects of our lives together. By cultivating gratitude, we can develop a mindset of love and patience, seeking to build a relationship that is grounded in trust, respect, and mutual support.

Contentment also involves being willing to let go of unrealistic expectations or desires, and to trust in God's provision and timing. In a relationship, it is easy to become focused on what is lacking or on what we wish were different. However, by cultivating contentment, we can learn to appreciate what we have, to trust in God's plan, and to respond with patience and understanding.

4. Seek God's Guidance and Strength

Cultivating patience in love requires us to seek God's guidance and strength. Patience is not something that we can develop on our own; it requires the work of the Holy Spirit in our hearts, transforming us into the image of Christ.

When we seek God's guidance and strength, we are acknowledging our dependence on Him and our need for His help. We are inviting Him into our relationship, asking Him to work in our hearts, to soften our hearts, and to align our hearts with His will. This reliance on God provides the foundation for patience, as we trust in His provision, timing, and plan.

Prayer is an essential part of seeking God's guidance and strength. Through prayer, we can express our needs, concerns, and desires to God, asking Him to help us develop the patience and understanding that we need in our relationship. By seeking God's guidance and strength, we can cultivate a spirit of patience, love, and grace, allowing our relationship to grow and flourish.

Conclusion

Patience and long-suffering are essential virtues for cultivating and maintaining a healthy and enduring romantic relationship. They are the foundation of love, trust, and mutual support, allowing us to navigate the challenges and difficulties of life together.

As we reflect on the words of Colossians 3:12-13, "Put on then, as God's chosen ones, holy and beloved, compassionate hearts, kindness, humility, meekness, and patience," let us be reminded of the importance of patience in our relationships. May we always seek to cultivate patience in our interactions, to bear with each other's flaws, and to build a relationship that is grounded in love, respect, and mutual support. And may we experience the fullness of love and life together, as we walk in faith, trust, and love, with patience as our guide.

Chapter 8: Sacrificial Love: A Christ-like Example

Introduction

Love is a word that carries profound depth and meaning, yet it is often used casually in our everyday lives. True love, however, goes beyond mere emotions or romantic gestures; it is rooted in sacrifice. The highest form of love is sacrificial love, the kind of love that willingly gives up everything for the sake of another. This love is epitomized by Jesus Christ, who made the ultimate sacrifice by laying down His life for humanity. In John 15:13, Jesus declares, "Greater love has no one than this: to lay down one's life for one's friends." This chapter delves into the concept of sacrificial love, exploring how Christ's example should shape and influence love in our relationships.

Understanding Sacrificial Love

Sacrificial love is a love that is willing to give up personal desires, comforts, and even life itself for the sake of another. It is a love that prioritizes the well-being, happiness, and spiritual growth of the other person, even at great personal cost. Sacrificial love is selfless, unconditional, and unwavering, reflecting the very heart of God.

In the Bible, the concept of sacrificial love is most vividly demonstrated in the life and death of Jesus Christ. Jesus' entire mission on earth was driven by sacrificial love—a love that sought to redeem, restore, and reconcile humanity to God. This love is not merely an abstract idea but is grounded in action, as seen in the ultimate sacrifice that Jesus made on the cross.

Sacrificial love is a foundational principle of the Christian faith. It is the kind of love that Jesus calls His followers to exhibit in their relationships with one another. This love goes beyond mere feelings or emotions; it is a deliberate choice to put the needs of others before our own, to serve selflessly, and to give without expecting anything in return.

1. The Nature of Sacrificial Love

The nature of sacrificial love is rooted in selflessness and humility. It is a love that does not seek its own gain but is willing to sacrifice for the benefit of others. Sacrificial love is characterized by a willingness to endure hardships, make sacrifices, and give of oneself without expecting anything in return.

In 1 Corinthians 13:4-7, the Apostle Paul describes the qualities of love, many of which are rooted in the concept of sacrifice: "Love is patient, love is kind. It does not envy, it does not boast, it is not proud. It does not dishonor others, it is not self-seeking, it is not easily angered, it keeps no record of wrongs. Love does not delight in evil but rejoices with the truth. It always protects, always trusts, always hopes, always perseveres."

These qualities of love reflect the selflessness and humility that are at the core of sacrificial love. It is a love that is patient and kind, even in the face of adversity. It is a love that does not seek its own advantage but prioritizes the well-being of others. It is a love that forgives, protects, and perseveres, even when it is difficult.

Sacrificial love is also characterized by a deep sense of commitment and dedication. It is a love that is willing to go the extra mile, to endure hardships, and to make sacrifices for the sake of the relationship. This kind of love is not based on feelings or emotions, which can be fleeting, but on a deep and unwavering commitment to the well-being of the other person.

2. The Ultimate Example of Sacrificial Love

The ultimate example of sacrificial love is found in the life and death of Jesus Christ. Jesus' entire mission on earth was driven by a deep, selfless love for humanity—a love that led Him to sacrifice His own life for the sake of others.

In Philippians 2:6-8, the Apostle Paul describes the sacrificial nature of Jesus' love: "Who, being in very nature God, did not consider equality with God something to be used to his own advantage; rather, he made himself nothing by taking the very nature of a servant, being made in human likeness. And being found in appearance as a man, he humbled himself by becoming obedient to death—even death on a cross!"

Jesus' sacrificial love is seen in His willingness to leave the glory of heaven, to take on human flesh, and to suffer and die for the sins of the world. This was not a sacrifice made out of obligation or duty, but out of pure, selfless love. Jesus' sacrifice on the cross was the ultimate expression of love—He laid down His life for His friends, and in doing so, He made a way for humanity to be reconciled to God.

Jesus' sacrificial love is not just an example for us to admire; it is a model for us to follow. In John 13:34, Jesus gives His disciples a new command: "Love one another. As I have loved you, so you must love one another." This command to love as Jesus loved is a call to sacrificial love—to be willing to give of ourselves, to make sacrifices, and to put the needs of others before our own.

Sacrificial Love in Romantic Relationships

Sacrificial love is not only foundational to our relationship with God, but it is also essential for cultivating and maintaining healthy, enduring romantic relationships. In the context of a romantic relationship, sacrificial love involves putting the needs and well-being of our partner above our own, serving selflessly, and making sacrifices for the sake of the relationship.

1. Sacrificial Love in Everyday Acts of Service

One of the most practical ways to demonstrate sacrificial love in a romantic relationship is through everyday acts of service. These acts of service may seem small or insignificant, but they are powerful expressions of love that can strengthen the bond between partners and create a foundation of trust and mutual respect.

Acts of service can take many forms, depending on the needs and preferences of your partner. It could be something as simple as making them breakfast in the morning, helping with household chores, or offering a listening ear after a long day. It could also involve more significant acts of service, such as supporting them during a challenging time, sacrificing your own time or resources to help them achieve a goal, or simply being there for them when they need you the most.

The key to sacrificial love in everyday acts of service is the willingness to put your partner's needs and desires above your own. It involves being attentive to their needs, going out of your way to make their life easier or more enjoyable, and doing so without expecting anything in return. These acts of service are powerful expressions of love because they demonstrate a selfless commitment to your partner's well-being and happiness.

2. Sacrificial Love in Times of Conflict and Disagreement

Conflict and disagreement are inevitable in any relationship. However, how we handle these conflicts can either strengthen or weaken the relationship.

Sacrificial love is essential in times of conflict because it involves putting the relationship above the need to be right, to win an argument, or to prove a point.

Sacrificial love in times of conflict involves being willing to listen, to understand your partner's perspective, and to work together to find a resolution. It requires humility, patience, and a willingness to forgive. Rather than focusing on your own desires or needs, sacrificial love involves prioritizing the health and well-being of the relationship.

One of the most powerful examples of sacrificial love in times of conflict is the willingness to forgive. Forgiveness is a crucial component of any healthy relationship, and it is an act of sacrificial love. It involves letting go of hurt, anger, and resentment, and choosing to extend grace and forgiveness to your partner, even when they have wronged you. This kind of forgiveness is not easy, but it is a powerful demonstration of sacrificial love.

Sacrificial love in times of conflict also involves being willing to make compromises for the sake of the relationship. There will be times when both partners have different opinions, desires, or preferences. Sacrificial love involves being willing to compromise, to put your partner's needs above your own, and to find a solution that benefits the relationship as a whole.

3. Sacrificial Love in Supporting Each Other's Growth

Another important aspect of sacrificial love in a romantic relationship is supporting each other's growth, both individually and as a couple. This involves being willing to make sacrifices, to invest time and energy into your partner's growth, and to prioritize their well-being and happiness.

Supporting your partner's growth may involve making sacrifices in your own life, such as giving up certain activities or pursuits to support your partner in achieving their goals. It may also involve being willing to challenge and encourage your partner to grow, even when it is difficult or uncomfortable.

Sacrificial love in supporting each other's growth also involves being willing to make sacrifices for the sake of the relationship. This may involve making changes in your own life, such as addressing personal issues or habits that may be negatively affecting the relationship. It may also involve being willing to make compromises, to prioritize the relationship over personal desires or goals, and to invest time and energy into building a strong and healthy relationship.

The key to sacrificial love in supporting each other's growth is the willingness to put your partner's needs and well-being above your own. It involves being selfless, humble, and committed to your partner's growth and happiness, even when it requires personal sacrifice.

4. Sacrificial Love in Times of Suffering and Hardship

Suffering and hardship are inevitable in life, and they can put a significant strain on a relationship. However, sacrificial love is essential in times of suffering because it involves being willing to endure hardship, to support your partner through difficult times, and to prioritize their well-being above your own.

Sacrificial love in times of suffering involves being present, supportive, and compassionate with your partner. It requires a willingness to bear with their pain, to provide comfort and understanding, and to walk through the difficulties together. Rather than focusing on your own needs or desires, sacrificial love involves prioritizing your partner's well-being and supporting them through the challenges they face.

One of the most powerful examples of sacrificial love in times of suffering is the willingness to make sacrifices for the sake of your partner's well-being. This may involve making changes in your own life, such as adjusting your schedule or priorities to be there for your partner, or it may involve making financial or other sacrifices to support your partner through a difficult time.

Sacrificial love in times of suffering also involves being willing to endure hardship for the sake of the relationship. This may involve enduring difficult circumstances, such as financial difficulties, health issues, or other challenges, with patience and grace. It may also involve being willing to make sacrifices for the sake of the relationship, such as giving up certain desires or goals to support your partner or to strengthen the relationship.

By exercising sacrificial love in times of suffering and hardship, you can strengthen your relationship, deepen your trust in God, and find hope and strength in His promises.

The Challenges of Sacrificial Love

While sacrificial love is essential for cultivating and maintaining a healthy and enduring romantic relationship, it is not without its challenges. Sacrificial love requires a deep sense of commitment, selflessness, and humility, and it can be difficult to sustain over the long term.

1. The Challenge of Selflessness

One of the biggest challenges of sacrificial love is the requirement of selflessness. In a culture that often prioritizes individual desires and personal fulfillment, sacrificial love challenges us to put the needs of others above our own, to prioritize the well-being of the relationship, and to serve selflessly.

Selflessness requires a willingness to let go of our own desires, preferences, and goals for the sake of the relationship. It involves being willing to make sacrifices, to put our partner's needs above our own, and to serve with humility and love.

However, selflessness is not easy, and it can be challenging to sustain over the long term. It requires a deep sense of commitment, a willingness to die to self, and a reliance on God's strength and guidance. It also requires a deep understanding of the nature of love and the importance of putting others before ourselves.

2. The Challenge of Humility

Another challenge of sacrificial love is the requirement of humility. Humility involves recognizing our own limitations, weaknesses, and need for growth. It involves being willing to admit when we are wrong, to seek forgiveness, and to prioritize the relationship over our own pride or ego.

Humility also involves being willing to serve, to put the needs of our partner above our own, and to approach the relationship with a spirit of love and grace. It requires a willingness to make sacrifices, to endure hardships, and to prioritize the well-being of the relationship over our own desires.

However, humility is not easy, and it can be challenging to sustain over the long term. It requires a deep sense of commitment, a willingness to put others before ourselves, and a reliance on God's strength and guidance.

3. The Challenge of Endurance

Sacrificial love requires endurance, especially in the face of challenges, difficulties, and hardships. Endurance involves a willingness to persevere, to remain steadfast in our love and commitment, even when it is difficult or uncomfortable.

Endurance is essential for maintaining a healthy and enduring romantic relationship. It involves a willingness to endure hardship, to support our partner through difficult times, and to prioritize the well-being of the relationship over our own desires.

However, endurance is not easy, and it can be challenging to sustain over the long term. It requires a deep sense of commitment, a willingness to make sacrifices, and a reliance on God's strength and guidance.

4. The Challenge of Forgiveness

Forgiveness is a crucial component of sacrificial love, but it is also one of the most challenging. Forgiveness involves letting go of hurt, anger, and resentment, and choosing to extend grace and forgiveness to our partner, even when they have wronged us.

Forgiveness is essential for maintaining a healthy and enduring romantic relationship. It involves a willingness to let go of past hurts, to seek reconciliation, and to prioritize the well-being of the relationship over our own desires.

However, forgiveness is not easy, and it can be challenging to sustain over the long term. It requires a deep sense of commitment, a willingness to let go of the need to be right, and a reliance on God's strength and guidance.

The Rewards of Sacrificial Love

While sacrificial love is not without its challenges, it also comes with great rewards. Sacrificial love has the power to transform relationships, to deepen our connection with God and with each other, and to create a foundation of trust, respect, and mutual support.

1. The Reward of Deepened Connection

One of the greatest rewards of sacrificial love is the deepened connection it creates between partners. Sacrificial love fosters a sense of trust, respect, and mutual support, allowing both partners to feel valued, loved, and supported.

This deepened connection creates a foundation for a healthy and enduring relationship, allowing both partners to navigate the challenges and difficulties of life together with confidence and hope.

2. The Reward of Spiritual Growth

Sacrificial love also fosters spiritual growth, both individually and as a couple. When we practice sacrificial love, we are aligning our hearts and minds with God's will, creating a sense of shared vision and direction.

This spiritual growth fosters a sense of maturity, as both partners learn to trust in God's guidance, to rely on His strength, and to grow in their love for Him and for each other.

3. The Reward of Emotional Intimacy

Sacrificial love also fosters emotional intimacy, allowing both partners to connect on a deeper level and to share their thoughts, feelings, and desires with each other.

This emotional intimacy creates a sense of closeness and trust, allowing both partners to feel valued, loved, and supported.

4. The Reward of Lasting Love

Finally, sacrificial love creates a foundation for lasting love. When we practice sacrificial love, we are building a relationship that is grounded in trust, respect, and mutual support.

This lasting love creates a sense of stability and security, allowing both partners to navigate the challenges and difficulties of life together with confidence and hope.

Conclusion

Sacrificial love is essential for cultivating and maintaining a healthy and enduring romantic relationship. It is a love that is willing to give up personal desires, comforts, and even life itself for the sake of another. Sacrificial love is selfless, unconditional, and unwavering, reflecting the very heart of God.

As we reflect on the words of John 15:13, "Greater love has no one than this: to lay down one's life for one's friends," let us be reminded of the importance of sacrificial love in our relationships. May we always seek to practice sacrificial love in our interactions, to bear with each other's flaws, and to build a relationship that is grounded in love, respect, and mutual support. And may we experience the fullness of love and life together, as we walk in faith, trust, and love, with sacrificial love as our guide.

Chapter 9: Love's Role in Spiritual Growth

Introduction

Love is a powerful force that shapes our lives, our relationships, and our spiritual journey. It is through love that we experience the fullness of life, and it is love that draws us closer to God and to one another. In the context of a loving relationship, love has the potential to be a profound catalyst for spiritual growth, helping each partner to mature in their faith, to draw closer to God, and to become more like Christ. The Apostle Paul, in his letter to the Ephesians, emphasizes the importance of love in spiritual growth: "Speaking the truth in love, we will grow to become in every respect the mature body of him who is the head, that is, Christ" (Ephesians 4:15-16). This chapter explores how a loving relationship can contribute to spiritual growth, examining the ways in which love can help each partner to grow closer to God and to strengthen their faith.

The Connection Between Love and Spiritual Growth

Spiritual growth is the process of becoming more like Christ, growing in our understanding of God, and deepening our relationship with Him. It is a lifelong journey that involves transformation, renewal, and the cultivation of virtues such as love, patience, humility, and faith. In this journey, love plays a central role. Love is not only the greatest commandment but also the foundation of spiritual growth. It is through love that we are able to reflect the character of Christ, to build meaningful relationships, and to experience the fullness of life in God.

In a loving relationship, love becomes the driving force that shapes the spiritual journey of each partner. A relationship that is grounded in love creates an environment where both partners can grow in their faith, support each other in their spiritual journey, and draw closer to God. Love in a relationship provides the foundation for spiritual growth by fostering trust, intimacy, and mutual support, all of which are essential for deepening one's relationship with God.

1. Love as a Reflection of God's Character

The first and most fundamental way that love contributes to spiritual growth is by reflecting the character of God. God is love (1 John 4:8), and His love is the source of all love. When we love others, we are reflecting the character of God and participating in His divine nature. This reflection of God's character is not only a powerful witness to the world but also a means of spiritual growth for ourselves.

In a loving relationship, love becomes a way of experiencing and expressing the character of God. When we love our partner with a selfless, sacrificial love, we are embodying the love of Christ and allowing His love to flow through us. This love is transformative, not only for our partner but also for ourselves. As we love others with the love of Christ, we are drawn closer to God, and our relationship with Him is deepened.

Love also reflects the character of God in the way it transforms us. Love is a powerful force that shapes our character, molding us into the image of Christ. When we love others, we are allowing God to work in us, to transform us, and to make us more like Him. This transformation is a key aspect of spiritual growth, as it involves the renewal of our minds, the cultivation of virtues, and the deepening of our relationship with God.

2. Love as a Catalyst for Spiritual Maturity

Love is not only a reflection of God's character but also a catalyst for spiritual maturity. Spiritual maturity is the process of growing in our faith, becoming more like Christ, and deepening our relationship with God. It is a journey of transformation, renewal, and growth, and love plays a central role in this journey.

In a loving relationship, love provides the foundation for spiritual maturity by fostering an environment of trust, intimacy, and mutual support. These elements are essential for spiritual growth, as they create a space where both partners can be vulnerable, honest, and open about their spiritual journey. In this environment, both partners can support each other in their spiritual growth, encouraging each other, challenging each other, and holding each other accountable.

Love also fosters spiritual maturity by providing the motivation to grow in our faith. When we love someone deeply, we are motivated to become the best version of ourselves, to grow in our faith, and to deepen our relationship with God. This motivation is not only for our own benefit but also for the benefit of our partner and our relationship. As we grow in our faith and become more like Christ, we are better able to love and support our partner, and our relationship becomes a reflection of God's love and grace.

3. Love as a Means of Experiencing God's Grace

Another important way that love contributes to spiritual growth is by providing a means of experiencing God's grace. Grace is the unmerited favor of God, the love and mercy that He extends to us even though we do not deserve it. Grace is at the heart of the Christian faith, and it is through grace that we are saved, transformed, and made new.

In a loving relationship, love becomes a means of experiencing and extending God's grace. When we love our partner with a selfless, sacrificial love, we are embodying the grace of God and allowing His grace to flow through us. This experience of grace is transformative, not only for our partner but also for ourselves. As we experience and extend God's grace in our relationship, we are drawn closer to God, and our relationship with Him is deepened.

Love also provides a means of experiencing God's grace in the way it helps us to forgive and be forgiven. Forgiveness is a key aspect of grace, and it is essential for maintaining a healthy and enduring relationship. When we forgive our partner, we are extending God's grace to them, and when we are forgiven, we are experiencing God's grace ourselves. This experience of grace is transformative, as it helps us to grow in our understanding of God's love and mercy and to deepen our relationship with Him.

4. Love as a Source of Strength and Support

Love is also a source of strength and support in the spiritual journey. The Christian life is not easy; it involves challenges, trials, and difficulties. In these times, love provides the strength and support that we need to persevere, to remain steadfast in our faith, and to continue growing in our relationship with God.

In a loving relationship, love provides a source of strength and support by creating a space where both partners can lean on each other, support each other, and encourage each other in their spiritual journey. This support is essential for spiritual growth, as it helps both partners to remain steadfast in their faith, to persevere through challenges, and to continue growing in their relationship with God.

Love also provides a source of strength and support in the way it helps us to bear with each other's weaknesses and flaws. In any relationship, there will be times when one partner is struggling, whether it is with doubt, fear, or sin. In these times, love provides the strength and support to bear with each other's weaknesses, to offer grace and understanding, and to help each other grow in their faith.

5. Love as a Reflection of Christ's Sacrifice

One of the most powerful ways that love contributes to spiritual growth is by reflecting the sacrifice of Christ. Jesus' entire mission on earth was driven by sacrificial love—a love that led Him to lay down His life for the sake of humanity. This sacrificial love is the ultimate expression of love, and it is a model for how we should love others.

In a loving relationship, love becomes a reflection of Christ's sacrifice by providing a means of selfless, sacrificial love. When we love our partner with a selfless, sacrificial love, we are embodying the love of Christ and allowing His love to flow through us. This sacrificial love is transformative, not only for our partner but also for ourselves. As we love others with the love of Christ, we are drawn closer to God, and our relationship with Him is deepened.

Sacrificial love also contributes to spiritual growth by helping us to die to ourselves and to live for Christ. The Christian life involves a process of dying to self, of letting go of our own desires, and of living for Christ. This process is not easy, but it is essential for spiritual growth. In a loving relationship, sacrificial love helps us to die to ourselves, to put our partner's needs above our own, and to live for Christ. This process of dying to self is transformative, as it helps us to grow in our relationship with God and to become more like Christ.

The Role of Love in Supporting Each Other's Spiritual Growth

In a loving relationship, love plays a central role in supporting each other's spiritual growth. This support is essential for maintaining a healthy and enduring relationship, as it helps both partners to grow in their faith, to deepen their relationship with God, and to become more like Christ.

1. Encouraging Each Other in Faith

One of the most important ways that love supports each other's spiritual growth is by providing encouragement in faith. Encouragement is a powerful force that helps to build up, strengthen, and support others in their spiritual journey. In a loving relationship, encouragement is essential for helping both partners to grow in their faith, to remain steadfast in their relationship with God, and to continue growing in their spiritual maturity.

Encouragement in faith can take many forms, depending on the needs and preferences of each partner. It could be something as simple as offering a kind word or a prayer, or it could involve more significant acts of support, such as participating in a Bible study together, attending church together, or offering spiritual guidance and wisdom.

The key to encouragement in faith is the willingness to support and build up each other in the spiritual journey. It involves being attentive to each other's needs, offering support and encouragement when it is needed, and being willing to walk alongside each other in the journey of faith.

2. Holding Each Other Accountable

Another important way that love supports each other's spiritual growth is by providing accountability. Accountability is the process of holding each other responsible for their actions, decisions, and growth in the spiritual journey. It is an essential aspect of spiritual growth, as it helps to keep us on track, to challenge us to grow, and to support us in our relationship with God.

In a loving relationship, accountability involves being willing to speak the truth in love, to challenge each other to grow, and to hold each other responsible for their actions and decisions. This process is not always easy, but it is essential for spiritual growth, as it helps both partners to remain steadfast in their faith, to grow in their relationship with God, and to become more like Christ.

Accountability also involves being willing to offer grace and forgiveness when needed. In any relationship, there will be times when one partner falls short, whether it is in their actions, decisions, or growth in the spiritual journey. In these times, accountability involves being willing to offer grace and forgiveness, to support each other in the process of growth and change, and to continue walking together in the journey of faith.

3. Praying for Each Other

Prayer is one of the most powerful ways that love supports each other's spiritual growth. Prayer is the means by which we communicate with God, seek His guidance and strength, and intercede for others. In a loving relationship, prayer is essential for supporting each other's spiritual growth, as it provides a means of lifting each other up before God, seeking His guidance and strength, and interceding for each other's needs and desires.

Praying for each other is a powerful expression of love, as it involves lifting up the needs, desires, and struggles of our partner before God. This act of prayer is transformative, not only for our partner but also for ourselves. As we pray for our partner, we are drawn closer to God, our relationship with Him is deepened, and our love for our partner is strengthened.

Prayer also provides a means of seeking God's guidance and strength in the spiritual journey. In a loving relationship, both partners will face challenges, trials, and difficulties in their spiritual journey. In these times, prayer provides a means of seeking God's guidance, strength, and support, and of walking together in the journey of faith.

4. Studying the Word of God Together

Studying the Word of God together is another important way that love supports each other's spiritual growth. The Bible is the inspired Word of God, and it is through the study of Scripture that we grow in our understanding of God, deepen our relationship with Him, and become more like Christ. In a loving relationship, studying the Word of God together provides a means of growing together in faith, of deepening our relationship with God, and of supporting each other in the spiritual journey.

Studying the Word of God together can take many forms, depending on the needs and preferences of each partner. It could involve participating in a Bible study together, reading and discussing Scripture together, or simply sharing insights and reflections on God's Word. The key is the willingness to grow together in the knowledge and love of God, and to support each other in the process of spiritual growth.

Studying the Word of God together also provides a means of applying the truths of Scripture to our relationship. The Bible is filled with wisdom and guidance for relationships, and as we study God's Word together, we can apply these truths to our own relationship, building a foundation of love, trust, and mutual support.

5. Serving Together

Serving together is another powerful way that love supports each other's spiritual growth. Service is a central aspect of the Christian life, as it involves putting the needs of others above our own and following the example of Christ, who came not to be served but to serve (Mark 10:45). In a loving relationship, serving together provides a means of growing together in faith, of deepening our relationship with God, and of supporting each other in the spiritual journey.

Serving together can take many forms, depending on the needs and preferences of each partner. It could involve volunteering together at a local church or community organization, participating in a mission trip, or simply serving each other in everyday acts of love and kindness. The key is the willingness to serve together, to put the needs of others above our own, and to follow the example of Christ in our relationship.

Serving together also provides a means of growing in humility, selflessness, and love. Service requires a willingness to put others first, to make sacrifices, and to follow the example of Christ. As we serve together, we grow in these virtues, becoming more like Christ and deepening our relationship with God and with each other.

Overcoming Challenges in Love and Spiritual Growth

While love plays a central role in supporting each other's spiritual growth, it is not without its challenges. The journey of spiritual growth is not easy, and there will be times when both partners face challenges, trials, and difficulties in their relationship and in their spiritual journey.

1. Dealing with Spiritual Differences

One of the challenges that may arise in a loving relationship is dealing with spiritual differences. These differences may include differences in beliefs, practices, or levels of spiritual maturity. These differences can create tension and conflict in the relationship, making it difficult to support each other in the spiritual journey.

Dealing with spiritual differences requires a willingness to listen, to understand each other's perspectives, and to find common ground. It involves being willing to respect each other's beliefs and practices, and to support each other in the journey of faith, even when there are differences.

Dealing with spiritual differences also involves being willing to grow together in the knowledge and love of God. This may involve participating in a Bible study together, seeking guidance from a spiritual mentor, or simply spending time in prayer and reflection together. The key is the willingness to grow together in faith, to support each other in the journey of faith, and to build a foundation of love and trust.

2. Navigating Spiritual Dry Spells

Another challenge that may arise in the journey of spiritual growth is navigating spiritual dry spells. A spiritual dry spell is a period of time when a person feels distant from God, lacks spiritual enthusiasm, or struggles to connect with God in prayer or worship. These dry spells can be difficult to navigate, as they can create feelings of doubt, discouragement, and frustration.

Navigating spiritual dry spells in a loving relationship requires a willingness to support each other through these difficult times. It involves being patient, understanding, and compassionate with each other, and offering encouragement and support when it is needed.

Navigating spiritual dry spells also involves being willing to seek God together. This may involve participating in a Bible study together, spending time in prayer and reflection together, or seeking guidance from a spiritual mentor. The key is the willingness to support each other in the journey of faith, to trust in God's guidance, and to persevere through the difficult times.

3. Balancing Personal and Spiritual Growth

Another challenge that may arise in the journey of spiritual growth is balancing personal and spiritual growth. The Christian life involves a process of personal growth, as we seek to become the best version of ourselves, and spiritual growth, as we seek to grow in our relationship with God. Balancing these two aspects of growth can be challenging, as they often require different approaches and priorities.

Balancing personal and spiritual growth in a loving relationship requires a willingness to prioritize both aspects of growth, and to support each other in the process. It involves being attentive to each other's needs and desires, and being willing to make sacrifices for the sake of the relationship.

Balancing personal and spiritual growth also involves being willing to grow together in faith. This may involve participating in a Bible study together, seeking guidance from a spiritual mentor, or simply spending time in prayer and reflection together. The key is the willingness to support each other in the journey of faith, to prioritize both aspects of growth, and to build a foundation of love and trust.

The Rewards of Love and Spiritual Growth

While the journey of spiritual growth is not easy, it is filled with great rewards. Love plays a central role in supporting each other's spiritual growth, and as we grow together in faith, we experience the fullness of life in God.

1. The Reward of Deepened Connection

One of the greatest rewards of love and spiritual growth is the deepened connection it creates between partners. As we grow together in faith, we build a foundation of love, trust, and mutual support, creating a space where both partners feel valued, loved, and supported.

This deepened connection creates a foundation for a healthy and enduring relationship, allowing both partners to navigate the challenges and difficulties of life together with confidence and hope.

2. The Reward of Spiritual Maturity

Love and spiritual growth also foster spiritual maturity, both individually and as a couple. As we grow together in faith, we become more like Christ, deepening our relationship with God and cultivating virtues such as love, patience, humility, and faith.

This spiritual maturity is a key aspect of the Christian life, as it involves the process of becoming more like Christ and deepening our relationship with God.

3. The Reward of Emotional Intimacy

Love and spiritual growth also foster emotional intimacy, allowing both partners to connect on a deeper level and to share their thoughts, feelings, and desires with each other.

This emotional intimacy creates a sense of closeness and trust, allowing both partners to feel valued, loved, and supported.

4. The Reward of Lasting Love

Finally, love and spiritual growth create a foundation for lasting love. As we grow together in faith, we build a relationship that is grounded in trust, respect, and mutual support, creating a space where both partners feel valued, loved, and supported.

This lasting love creates a sense of stability and security, allowing both partners to navigate the challenges and difficulties of life together with confidence and hope.

Conclusion

Love plays a central role in spiritual growth, providing the foundation for a healthy and enduring relationship. It is through love that we grow in our faith, deepen our relationship with God, and become more like Christ. Love supports each other's spiritual growth by providing encouragement, accountability, and prayer, and by fostering a sense of trust, intimacy, and mutual support.

As we reflect on the words of Ephesians 4:15-16, "Speaking the truth in love, we will grow to become in every respect the mature body of him who is the head, that is, Christ," let us be reminded of the importance of love in our relationships and in our spiritual growth. May we always seek to love and support each other in the journey of faith, to grow together in the knowledge and love of God, and to experience the fullness of life in Him. And may we experience the rewards of love and spiritual growth, as we walk in faith, trust, and love, with Christ as our guide.

Chapter 10: The Covenant of Marriage: A Reflection of God's Covenant

Introduction

Marriage is one of the most profound and sacred institutions in human existence. It is not merely a social contract or a legal agreement but a covenant—a binding promise that reflects the very nature of God's relationship with His people. The covenant of marriage is designed to be a reflection of God's covenant with humanity, marked by love, faithfulness, and permanence. This sacred union is meant to embody the depth of God's love, the seriousness of His commitment, and the enduring nature of His promises. In Malachi 2:14, the prophet reminds us of the seriousness of this covenant: "The Lord was witness between you and the wife of your youth, to whom you have been faithless, though she is your companion and your wife by covenant." This chapter delves into the theological significance of the covenant of marriage, exploring how it serves as a reflection of God's covenant with His people and emphasizing the sacredness and permanence of marital love.

Understanding the Covenant of Marriage

The concept of covenant is central to the Bible and to the understanding of God's relationship with humanity. A covenant, in biblical terms, is a solemn agreement or promise between two parties, often sealed with a sign or ritual. It is not merely a contract that can be broken or altered, but a binding, unbreakable promise that carries deep spiritual and relational significance.

Marriage, according to Scripture, is a covenant—a sacred vow made between a man and a woman before God. It is an institution ordained by God, intended to reflect the divine relationship between God and His people. The covenant of marriage is marked by mutual love, faithfulness, and commitment, and it is designed to be a lifelong union that mirrors the unbreakable bond between God and His covenant people.

1. The Biblical Foundation of the Marriage Covenant

The biblical foundation of the marriage covenant is established in the very beginning of Scripture, in the creation account of Genesis. In Genesis 2:24, we read, "Therefore a man shall leave his father and mother and be joined to his wife, and they shall become one flesh." This verse lays the foundation for the covenant of marriage, emphasizing the unity, permanence, and sacredness of the marital bond.

The concept of "one flesh" is significant in understanding the covenant of marriage. It signifies the deep, intimate union that takes place in marriage, where two individuals become one in body, mind, and spirit. This union is not merely physical but encompasses the entirety of the relationship, including emotional, spiritual, and relational aspects. The "one flesh" union in marriage reflects the unity and oneness that God desires in His relationship with His people.

Throughout the Old and New Testaments, marriage is consistently portrayed as a covenant. In Malachi 2:14, the prophet refers to marriage as a covenant, emphasizing the seriousness of marital vows and the consequences of breaking them. In the New Testament, Jesus reaffirms the covenantal nature of marriage in Matthew 19:6, where He says, "So they are no longer two, but one flesh. Therefore what God has joined together, let no one separate." Here, Jesus highlights the permanence of the marriage covenant, underscoring that it is a divine union that should not be broken.

2. The Sacredness of the Marriage Covenant

The covenant of marriage is sacred because it is ordained by God and reflects His holy and unchanging nature. It is a covenant that is entered into before God, with Him as the ultimate witness and authority. The sacredness of marriage is rooted in the fact that it is a divine institution, designed by God to reflect His character and His relationship with His people.

The sacredness of the marriage covenant is also evident in the vows that are exchanged during the wedding ceremony. These vows are not just promises made to one another but are solemn commitments made before God. The traditional marriage vows often include phrases such as "to have and to hold, from this day forward, for better or for worse, for richer or for poorer, in sickness and in health, to love and to cherish, until death do us part." These vows reflect the seriousness and permanence of the marriage covenant, as well as the commitment to love and faithfulness that is required in marriage.

The sacredness of the marriage covenant also means that it should be treated with the utmost respect and reverence. Marriage is not something to be entered into lightly or casually; it is a holy and sacred union that requires careful consideration, prayer, and preparation. The decision to marry should be based on a deep understanding of the covenantal nature of marriage and a commitment to honor and uphold the sacred vows that are made.

3. The Permanence of the Marriage Covenant

The covenant of marriage is designed to be permanent, reflecting the unbreakable nature of God's covenant with His people. In a world where relationships are often viewed as temporary and disposable, the biblical concept of the permanence of marriage stands in stark contrast. Marriage, according to Scripture, is intended to be a lifelong union, marked by faithfulness, commitment, and enduring love.

The permanence of the marriage covenant is emphasized throughout Scripture. In Malachi 2:16, God declares, "I hate divorce," highlighting the seriousness with which He views the breaking of the marriage covenant. In Matthew 19:6, Jesus underscores the permanence of marriage, stating, "Therefore what God has joined together, let no one separate." These passages make it clear that marriage is intended to be a lifelong commitment, reflecting the enduring nature of God's covenant with His people.

The permanence of the marriage covenant also means that it requires ongoing effort, commitment, and perseverance. Marriage is not always easy, and there will be times of difficulty, conflict, and challenge. However, the covenantal nature of marriage calls for a steadfast commitment to work through these challenges, to seek reconciliation and healing, and to remain faithful to the vows that were made.

The permanence of marriage is also a reflection of God's faithfulness. Just as God remains faithful to His covenant with His people, even when they are unfaithful, so too are married couples called to remain faithful to one another, even in times of difficulty. The commitment to remain faithful in marriage, despite challenges and hardships, is a powerful reflection of the steadfast love and faithfulness of God.

4. The Covenant of Marriage as a Reflection of God's Covenant

The covenant of marriage is not only a sacred and permanent union but also a reflection of God's covenant with His people. Throughout Scripture, the relationship between God and His people is often portrayed as a marriage, with God as the faithful husband and His people as the bride. This imagery is most vividly seen in the book of Hosea, where God's relationship with Israel is depicted as a marriage, marked by both love and faithfulness, as well as betrayal and forgiveness.

In Ephesians 5:25-27, the Apostle Paul draws a parallel between the marriage relationship and the relationship between Christ and the Church: "Husbands, love your wives, just as Christ loved the church and gave himself up for her to make her holy, cleansing her by the washing with water through the word, and to present her to himself as a radiant church, without stain or wrinkle or any other blemish, but holy and blameless." Here, Paul highlights the sacrificial love that Christ has for the Church, and he calls husbands to love their wives in the same way. This passage underscores the idea that marriage is a reflection of the covenant between Christ and the Church, marked by love, sacrifice, and a commitment to holiness.

The covenant of marriage, therefore, is not just about the relationship between a husband and wife; it is also a reflection of the divine relationship between God and His people. Just as God's covenant with His people is marked by faithfulness, love, and commitment, so too should the marriage covenant be characterized by these qualities. Marriage, when lived out according to God's design, becomes a powerful testimony to the world of the depth of God's love and the seriousness of His covenant.

The Responsibilities of the Marriage Covenant

The covenant of marriage carries with it significant responsibilities. These responsibilities are not merely obligations but are opportunities to reflect the character of God and to grow in love, faithfulness, and holiness. The responsibilities of the marriage covenant include love, faithfulness, mutual respect, and a commitment to the growth and well-being of one's spouse.

1. The Responsibility of Love

The primary responsibility of the marriage covenant is love. This love is not merely a feeling or emotion but is an action—a deliberate choice to put the needs and well-being of one's spouse above one's own. In 1 Corinthians 13:4-7, the Apostle Paul provides a beautiful description of the kind of love that should characterize the marriage relationship: "Love is patient, love is kind. It does not envy, it does not boast, it is not proud. It does not dishonor others, it is not self-seeking, it is not easily angered, it keeps no record of wrongs. Love does not delight in evil but rejoices with the truth. It always protects, always trusts, always hopes, always perseveres."

This passage highlights the selfless, sacrificial nature of love that should be at the heart of the marriage covenant. Love in marriage involves patience, kindness, humility, and a commitment to the well-being of one's spouse. It requires a willingness to forgive, to bear with one another's weaknesses, and to seek the best for one's spouse.

Love in marriage is also a reflection of God's love for His people. Just as God loves us with an unconditional, sacrificial love, so too are married couples called to love one another in the same way. This love is not based on feelings or circumstances but is rooted in a deep commitment to the covenant that was made before God.

2. The Responsibility of Faithfulness

Faithfulness is another key responsibility of the marriage covenant. Faithfulness in marriage involves a commitment to remain true to one's spouse, both physically and emotionally. It requires a steadfast commitment to the vows that were made and a determination to remain loyal, even in times of difficulty.

Faithfulness in marriage is a reflection of God's faithfulness to His covenant with His people. Throughout Scripture, God is portrayed as a faithful husband who remains true to His covenant, even when His people are unfaithful. In the book of Hosea, God's relationship with Israel is depicted as a marriage, with Israel's unfaithfulness likened to adultery. Despite Israel's unfaithfulness, God remains committed to His covenant, seeking to restore and redeem His people.

In the same way, married couples are called to remain faithful to one another, even in times of difficulty. This faithfulness is not just about avoiding physical infidelity but also involves emotional and relational faithfulness. It requires a commitment to nurture and protect the marriage relationship, to prioritize the needs of one's spouse, and to remain true to the vows that were made.

3. The Responsibility of Mutual Respect

Mutual respect is another important responsibility of the marriage covenant. Respect in marriage involves honoring and valuing one's spouse, recognizing their worth and dignity, and treating them with kindness and consideration. It requires a commitment to listen to one another, to communicate openly and honestly, and to seek to understand each other's needs and desires.

Mutual respect in marriage is a reflection of the respect that God has for His people. Throughout Scripture, God demonstrates His love and respect for His people by listening to their prayers, guiding them with wisdom, and treating them with kindness and compassion. In the same way, married couples are called to demonstrate respect for one another, recognizing the inherent worth and dignity of their spouse and treating them with the love and honor that they deserve.

Respect in marriage also involves a commitment to protect and cherish the marriage relationship. This includes protecting the relationship from outside influences, guarding against anything that could harm the marriage, and actively working to strengthen and nurture the relationship.

4. The Responsibility of Growth and Well-Being

The covenant of marriage also carries with it the responsibility to promote the growth and well-being of one's spouse. This involves a commitment to support one another's spiritual, emotional, and physical well-being, and to actively seek the growth and development of one's spouse.

Supporting each other's spiritual growth is a key aspect of the marriage covenant. This involves encouraging one another in the faith, praying together, studying Scripture together, and seeking to grow together in the knowledge and love of God. It also involves holding each other accountable in the spiritual journey, challenging each other to grow, and providing support and encouragement in times of difficulty.

Supporting each other's emotional and physical well-being is also an important responsibility of the marriage covenant. This involves being attentive to one another's needs, providing comfort and support in times of difficulty, and actively seeking the health and well-being of one's spouse. It also involves a commitment to work together to maintain a healthy and balanced lifestyle, to support each other's goals and aspirations, and to create a home environment that promotes peace, joy, and well-being.

The Challenges of Upholding the Marriage Covenant

While the covenant of marriage is a beautiful and sacred institution, it is not without its challenges. Upholding the marriage covenant requires ongoing effort, commitment, and perseverance, especially in the face of difficulties and challenges.

1. The Challenge of Conflict and Disagreement

One of the challenges of upholding the marriage covenant is dealing with conflict and disagreement. Conflict is inevitable in any relationship, and how it is handled can either strengthen or weaken the marriage covenant.

The key to dealing with conflict in marriage is to approach it with a spirit of love, humility, and respect. This involves being willing to listen to one another, to seek to understand each other's perspectives, and to work together to find a resolution. It also involves being willing to forgive, to let go of past hurts, and to seek reconciliation and healing.

Conflict in marriage can also be an opportunity for growth and strengthening the marriage covenant. When handled well, conflict can lead to greater understanding, deeper intimacy, and a stronger commitment to the marriage covenant.

2. The Challenge of Temptation and Unfaithfulness

Another challenge of upholding the marriage covenant is dealing with temptation and the potential for unfaithfulness. In a world where infidelity is often portrayed as acceptable or even desirable, remaining faithful to the marriage covenant can be challenging.

The key to dealing with temptation in marriage is to actively guard and protect the marriage relationship. This involves setting boundaries, being vigilant about potential threats to the marriage, and actively nurturing and strengthening the marriage relationship. It also involves a commitment to remain faithful, even in times of difficulty, and to seek help and support if needed.

Faithfulness in marriage is not just about avoiding physical infidelity but also involves emotional and relational faithfulness. This means being committed to nurturing and protecting the emotional bond with one's spouse, and avoiding anything that could harm or undermine the marriage relationship.

3. The Challenge of Maintaining the Marriage Covenant in Difficult Times

Another challenge of upholding the marriage covenant is maintaining the commitment to the covenant in difficult times. Marriage is not always easy, and there will be times of difficulty, conflict, and challenge. However, the covenantal nature of marriage calls for a steadfast commitment to work through these challenges, to seek reconciliation and healing, and to remain faithful to the vows that were made.

The key to maintaining the marriage covenant in difficult times is to remain committed to the covenant, even when it is difficult. This involves a willingness to work through challenges, to seek help and support if needed, and to actively nurture and protect the marriage relationship. It also involves a commitment to seek God's guidance and strength in the journey, trusting in His faithfulness and provision.

The Rewards of Upholding the Marriage Covenant

While upholding the marriage covenant can be challenging, it also comes with great rewards. When the marriage covenant is honored and upheld, it becomes a powerful reflection of God's love and faithfulness, and it creates a foundation for a healthy, enduring, and fulfilling relationship.

1. The Reward of Deepened Intimacy and Connection

One of the greatest rewards of upholding the marriage covenant is the deepened intimacy and connection that it creates between spouses. When the marriage covenant is honored, it creates a foundation of trust, respect, and mutual support, allowing both partners to feel valued, loved, and supported.

This deepened intimacy and connection create a foundation for a healthy and enduring relationship, allowing both partners to navigate the challenges and difficulties of life together with confidence and hope.

2. The Reward of Spiritual Growth and Maturity

Upholding the marriage covenant also fosters spiritual growth and maturity, both individually and as a couple. When the marriage covenant is honored, it creates a space for both partners to grow in their relationship with God, to deepen their understanding of His love and faithfulness, and to become more like Christ.

This spiritual growth and maturity are a key aspect of the Christian life, as they involve the process of becoming more like Christ and deepening our relationship with God.

3. The Reward of Lasting Love and Faithfulness

Finally, upholding the marriage covenant creates a foundation for lasting love and faithfulness. When the marriage covenant is honored, it creates a relationship that is grounded in trust, respect, and mutual support, allowing both partners to experience the fullness of love and life together.

This lasting love and faithfulness create a sense of stability and security, allowing both partners to navigate the challenges and difficulties of life together with confidence and hope.

Conclusion

The covenant of marriage is a sacred and permanent union, reflecting the very nature of God's relationship with His people. It is a covenant marked by love, faithfulness, and a commitment to growth and well-being. While upholding the marriage covenant can be challenging, it also comes with great rewards, including deepened intimacy and connection, spiritual growth and maturity, and lasting love and faithfulness.

As we reflect on the words of Malachi 2:14, "The Lord was witness between you and the wife of your youth, to whom you have been faithless, though she is your companion and your wife by covenant," let us be reminded of the sacredness and permanence of the marriage covenant. May we always seek to honor and uphold the marriage covenant, to love and support one another, and to reflect the love and faithfulness of God in our relationships. And may we experience the fullness of love and life together, as we walk in faith, trust, and love, with Christ as our guide.

Chapter 11: Hope in Love: A Future Together

Introduction

Hope is a powerful and essential component of love, particularly in the context of a committed relationship. It is the anchor that sustains us through the trials and uncertainties of life, providing a vision for the future and a source of strength in times of difficulty. In the Christian faith, hope is not a wishful thinking or a mere desire for good things to happen, but a confident expectation rooted in the promises of God. This kind of hope is especially important in a romantic relationship, where it shapes the way we view our future together and influences how we navigate the challenges we face. The Apostle Paul, in his letter to the Romans, emphasizes the significance of hope in the life of a believer: "For in this hope we were saved. Now hope that is seen is not hope. For who hopes for what he sees?" (Romans 8:24-25). This chapter will explore the theme of hope in love, focusing on the anticipation of a future together and how hope sustains a relationship through uncertainties.

The Nature of Hope in Love

Hope is a deeply spiritual and emotional concept that goes beyond simple optimism or positive thinking. It is a confident expectation that is grounded in faith and trust in God's promises. In the context of love and relationships, hope is the belief that despite the challenges and uncertainties of life, the future holds something good, something worth striving for and waiting for.

Hope in love is not blind optimism that ignores the difficulties and struggles of life. Rather, it is a realistic yet confident expectation that, with God's help, a couple can overcome obstacles and build a meaningful and fulfilling life together. This hope is rooted in the character of God, who is faithful, loving, and just, and who has promised to be with us through all the ups and downs of life.

1. Hope as a Confident Expectation

The first aspect of hope in love is that it is a confident expectation. This means that hope is not just a vague desire for things to turn out well, but a firm belief that, with God's help, the future will be good. This confidence is not based on our own abilities or circumstances, but on the character and promises of God.

In Romans 8:24-25, Paul reminds us that hope is something that is not yet seen. "For in this hope we were saved. Now hope that is seen is not hope. For who hopes for what he sees?" This verse highlights the idea that hope is about looking forward to something that is not yet realized, but that we trust will come to pass because of God's faithfulness. In a relationship, this kind of hope can sustain a couple through difficult times, helping them to keep their eyes on the future and to trust that God is at work, even when the present is challenging.

2. Hope as a Source of Strength

Another important aspect of hope in love is that it provides strength in times of difficulty. Life is full of challenges, and relationships are no exception. There will be times when things are difficult, when misunderstandings arise, when external pressures weigh heavily on the relationship, or when unforeseen circumstances test the bond between partners. In these times, hope can be a powerful source of strength and resilience.

Hope helps couples to endure difficult times because it gives them something to hold onto. It reminds them that the current struggles are not the end of the story, and that there is a future worth working toward. This hope can inspire patience, perseverance, and determination to work through difficulties rather than giving up.

Hope also provides strength by reminding couples that they are not alone in their struggles. God is with them, and His presence brings comfort, guidance, and support. This awareness of God's presence can help couples to face challenges with courage and to trust that, with His help, they can overcome whatever obstacles come their way.

3. Hope as a Vision for the Future

Hope in love also involves having a vision for the future. This vision is not just about what a couple wants to achieve or accomplish together, but about the kind of life they want to build, the values they want to uphold, and the legacy they want to leave behind. This vision is shaped by their faith, their love for each other, and their desire to honor God in their relationship.

Having a shared vision for the future is important because it gives a couple direction and purpose. It helps them to stay focused on what really matters and to make decisions that are in line with their long-term goals. This vision also provides motivation to keep moving forward, even when the journey is difficult.

A shared vision for the future also strengthens the bond between partners. When a couple is united in their vision for the future, they are more likely to support each other, to work together as a team, and to stay committed to their relationship. This shared vision can also help them to navigate differences and conflicts, as it reminds them of their common goals and the bigger picture.

Hope in the Face of Uncertainty

Uncertainty is a natural part of life, and it is something that every couple will face at some point in their relationship. Whether it is uncertainty about the future, about the direction of the relationship, or about external circumstances, it can be difficult to navigate these unknowns. However, hope can play a crucial role in helping couples to face uncertainty with faith and confidence.

1. Trusting in God's Sovereignty

The first key to navigating uncertainty with hope is to trust in God's sovereignty. As believers, we know that God is in control of all things, and that nothing happens outside of His will. This means that, even when we don't understand what is happening or why, we can trust that God has a plan and that He is working all things for our good (Romans 8:28).

Trusting in God's sovereignty allows us to let go of the need to control everything and to rest in the knowledge that He is in charge. This trust can bring peace and calm in the midst of uncertainty, and it can help couples to face the unknown with confidence and hope.

2. Holding onto God's Promises

Another key to navigating uncertainty with hope is to hold onto God's promises. The Bible is filled with promises that God has made to His people—promises of His presence, His provision, His guidance, and His love. These promises are a source of hope because they remind us that, no matter what happens, God is with us and He is for us.

In times of uncertainty, couples can find strength and encouragement by meditating on God's promises and by reminding each other of His faithfulness.

This practice can help them to stay focused on what is true and to resist the temptation to give in to fear or doubt.

Holding onto God's promises also involves trusting in His timing. There are times when we have to wait for God to fulfill His promises, and this waiting can be difficult. However, hope helps us to wait with patience and trust, knowing that God is faithful and that He will fulfill His promises in His perfect timing.

3. Embracing the Journey

Another important aspect of navigating uncertainty with hope is to embrace the journey. Life is a journey, and so is love. Along the way, there will be twists and turns, ups and downs, and unexpected detours. However, hope helps us to embrace the journey, to see it as an adventure, and to trust that God is leading us every step of the way.

Embracing the journey means being willing to step out in faith, even when we don't know what the future holds. It means being open to change, to growth, and to new possibilities. It also means trusting that God is with us on the journey, guiding us, and providing for us along the way.

When couples embrace the journey with hope, they are more likely to face challenges with a positive attitude and to see difficulties as opportunities for growth and learning. This mindset can strengthen their bond and deepen their love for each other.

4. Supporting Each Other through Uncertainty

Hope in the face of uncertainty is also about supporting each other through the unknowns. In a loving relationship, partners are called to be there for each other, to provide comfort and encouragement, and to walk alongside each other in the journey of life.

Supporting each other through uncertainty involves listening to each other's fears and concerns, offering reassurance and comfort, and reminding each other of God's faithfulness. It also involves praying together, seeking God's guidance together, and making decisions together in a spirit of unity and love.

When couples support each other through uncertainty, they are not only strengthening their relationship but also growing in their faith and trust in God. This mutual support can help them to face the unknowns with confidence and hope, knowing that they are not alone in the journey.

Hope in the Context of Commitment

Hope is closely tied to the concept of commitment in a relationship. Commitment is the decision to stay true to one's partner, to work through difficulties, and to build a life together. Hope is what sustains this commitment, giving couples the strength and motivation to keep going, even when the road is rough.

1. The Role of Hope in Sustaining Commitment

Hope plays a crucial role in sustaining commitment because it provides a vision for the future and a reason to keep going. When couples have hope for the future, they are more likely to stay committed to each other and to their relationship. This hope gives them the motivation to work through challenges, to invest in their relationship, and to stay true to their vows.

Hope also sustains commitment by reminding couples of the bigger picture. In the midst of difficulties, it can be easy to get caught up in the moment and to lose sight of the long-term goals. However, hope helps couples to stay focused on the future and to remember why they made the commitment in the first place.

2. Hope and the Power of Perseverance

Perseverance is a key aspect of commitment, and hope plays a vital role in fostering perseverance. Perseverance is the ability to keep going, even when things are tough, and to remain steadfast in the face of difficulties. It is about staying the course, even when the road is long and challenging.

Hope fosters perseverance by providing the strength and motivation to keep going. When couples have hope, they are more likely to persevere through difficulties, to work through conflicts, and to stay committed to each other. This perseverance is not just about enduring the difficult times but about growing through them and coming out stronger on the other side.

Perseverance is also about trusting in God's timing and plan. There are times when things don't happen as quickly as we would like or when the outcome is not what we expected. In these times, hope helps us to persevere, to trust that God is at work, and to keep moving forward in faith.

3. Hope and the Role of Patience

Patience is another important aspect of commitment, and hope plays a crucial role in fostering patience. Patience is the ability to wait, to be patient with each other, and to trust in God's timing. It is about being willing to wait for the good things that are to come and to trust that God is working in the midst of the waiting.

Hope fosters patience by reminding us that the future is worth waiting for. When couples have hope, they are more likely to be patient with each other, to give each other grace, and to trust that God is working in their relationship. This patience is not just about waiting passively but about actively trusting in God's plan and timing.

Patience is also about being willing to work through the process. Relationships take time to grow and develop, and there will be times when progress is slow. In these times, hope helps couples to be patient, to trust the process, and to keep working toward their goals.

4. Hope and the Importance of Faith

Faith is the foundation of hope, and it plays a crucial role in sustaining commitment. Faith is the belief that God is who He says He is and that He will do what He has promised. It is the trust that God is in control and that He is working all things for our good.

Hope is rooted in faith, and it is this faith that sustains commitment. When couples have faith in God, they are more likely to stay committed to each other and to their relationship. This faith gives them the strength to keep going, even when the road is rough, and the confidence to trust that God is working in their relationship.

Faith also helps couples to stay focused on the bigger picture. In the midst of difficulties, it can be easy to lose sight of God's plan and to focus on the immediate challenges. However, faith helps couples to stay focused on the future, to trust that God is in control, and to keep moving forward in faith.

Hope as a Foundation for a Future Together

Hope is not just about the present or the immediate future; it is also about the long-term vision for a life together. This vision is shaped by faith, love, and a commitment to building a life that honors God and reflects His love.

1. Building a Future Together

Building a future together is one of the most important aspects of a committed relationship. This future is not just about achieving goals or reaching milestones but about creating a life that reflects the values, beliefs, and vision that a couple shares.

Hope plays a crucial role in building a future together because it provides the vision and motivation to keep moving forward. When couples have hope for the future, they are more likely to work together, to support each other, and to stay committed to their relationship.

Building a future together also involves making decisions that are in line with the vision and goals that a couple shares. This requires communication, collaboration, and a willingness to work together to achieve common goals.

2. Hope and the Role of Vision in a Relationship

Vision is a key aspect of hope, and it plays a crucial role in building a future together. Vision is about having a clear picture of what a couple wants to achieve together, the kind of life they want to build, and the legacy they want to leave behind.

Hope fosters vision by providing the inspiration and motivation to keep moving forward. When couples have a shared vision for the future, they are more likely to stay focused on their goals, to work together as a team, and to stay committed to their relationship.

Vision is also about having a long-term perspective. In the midst of challenges, it can be easy to get caught up in the moment and to lose sight of the bigger picture. However, hope helps couples to stay focused on the future, to remember why they made the commitment in the first place, and to keep working toward their goals.

3. Hope and the Role of Faith in Building a Future Together

Faith is the foundation of hope, and it plays a crucial role in building a future together. Faith is about trusting that God is in control, that He has a plan for our lives, and that He is working all things for our good.

Hope is rooted in faith, and it is this faith that sustains a couple as they work toward their future together. When couples have faith in God, they are more likely to stay committed to each other, to trust in God's plan, and to keep moving forward in faith.

Faith also helps couples to stay focused on the bigger picture. In the midst of challenges, it can be easy to lose sight of God's plan and to focus on the immediate difficulties. However, faith helps couples to stay focused on the future, to trust that God is in control, and to keep moving forward in faith.

4. Hope and the Role of Perseverance in Building a Future Together

Perseverance is a key aspect of building a future together, and hope plays a crucial role in fostering perseverance. Perseverance is about staying the course, even when the road is rough, and remaining steadfast in the face of difficulties.

Hope fosters perseverance by providing the strength and motivation to keep going. When couples have hope for the future, they are more likely to persevere through difficulties, to work through conflicts, and to stay committed to each other.

Perseverance is also about trusting in God's timing and plan. There are times when things don't happen as quickly as we would like or when the outcome is not what we expected. In these times, hope helps us to persevere, to trust that God is at work, and to keep moving forward in faith.

The Rewards of Hope in Love

While the journey of hope in love is not always easy, it is filled with great rewards. Hope provides a foundation for a healthy, enduring, and fulfilling relationship, and it creates a vision for a future that is worth striving for.

1. The Reward of Deepened Intimacy and Connection

One of the greatest rewards of hope in love is the deepened intimacy and connection that it creates between partners. When couples have hope for the future, they are more likely to work together, to support each other, and to stay committed to their relationship.

This deepened intimacy and connection create a foundation for a healthy and enduring relationship, allowing both partners to navigate the challenges and difficulties of life together with confidence and hope.

2. The Reward of Spiritual Growth and Maturity

Hope in love also fosters spiritual growth and maturity, both individually and as a couple. When couples have hope for the future, they are more likely to trust in God's plan, to seek His guidance, and to grow in their faith.

This spiritual growth and maturity are a key aspect of the Christian life, as they involve the process of becoming more like Christ and deepening our relationship with God.

3. The Reward of Lasting Love and Commitment

Finally, hope in love creates a foundation for lasting love and commitment. When couples have hope for the future, they are more likely to stay committed to each other, to work through challenges, and to build a life together that honors God.

This lasting love and commitment create a sense of stability and security, allowing both partners to navigate the challenges and difficulties of life together with confidence and hope.

Conclusion

Hope in love is a powerful and essential component of a committed relationship. It provides the vision and motivation to keep moving forward, even when the road is rough, and it sustains a couple through the trials and uncertainties of life. Hope is not just about wishful thinking but is a confident expectation rooted in the promises of God.

As we reflect on the words of Romans 8:24-25, "For in this hope we were saved. Now hope that is seen is not hope. For who hopes for what he sees?" let us be reminded of the importance of hope in our relationships and in our journey of faith. May we always seek to hold onto hope, to trust in God's plan, and to build a future together that honors Him. And may we experience the fullness of love and life together, as we walk in faith, trust, and hope, with Christ as our guide.

Chapter 12: Love That Reflects God's Glory

Introduction

Love is at the heart of the Christian faith, and it is through love that we most clearly reflect the character and glory of God. In a world that is often darkened by selfishness, division, and hatred, a loving relationship stands out as a beacon of light, pointing others to the goodness and grace of God. Jesus himself emphasized the importance of letting our light shine before others so that they may see our good deeds and glorify our Father in heaven (Matthew 5:16). This chapter will explore how a loving relationship can reflect God's glory to the world, serving as a powerful testament to His goodness, grace, and transformative power.

The Concept of Reflecting God's Glory

To understand how a loving relationship can reflect God's glory, we must first grasp the concept of God's glory itself. In Scripture, the glory of God refers to the manifestation of His divine attributes—His holiness, righteousness, love, mercy, and power. God's glory is His intrinsic worth and majesty, made visible to creation. When we speak of reflecting God's glory, we mean living in such a way that others can see the character of God in us, and through us, be drawn to worship and glorify Him.

Reflecting God's glory is not limited to individual acts of piety or worship; it encompasses every aspect of our lives, including our relationships. In a loving relationship, when two people are committed to living out the principles of love, grace, forgiveness, and selflessness, they become a living testimony of God's character. Their relationship serves as a visible demonstration of God's love and goodness, inviting others to experience His glory for themselves.

1. The Purpose of Reflecting God's Glory in Relationships

One of the primary purposes of any relationship, particularly a romantic or marital relationship, is to reflect God's glory. God created human beings in His image, and He designed relationships to be a mirror of His love and faithfulness. When a couple loves each other with a selfless, sacrificial love, they are reflecting the very nature of God, who is love (1 John 4:8). This reflection of

God's character is not only for the benefit of the couple but also for the world around them.

In Matthew 5:16, Jesus calls His followers to let their light shine before others so that they may see their good deeds and glorify God. In the context of a loving relationship, this means living in such a way that others can see the love, grace, and forgiveness of God reflected in the way we treat our partner. Our relationships should be a testament to God's goodness, serving as a witness to those who do not yet know Him.

Reflecting God's glory in our relationships also has a transformative effect on those around us. When others see the love and grace of God lived out in our relationships, they are drawn to Him. Our relationships become a powerful tool for evangelism, as they demonstrate the reality of God's love and the difference that He makes in our lives.

2. The Role of Love in Reflecting God's Glory

Love is the foundation of any relationship that seeks to reflect God's glory. It is through love that we most clearly demonstrate the character of God, who is the source and embodiment of all love. In a loving relationship, when we love our partner with a selfless, sacrificial love, we are reflecting the love of God to the world.

The Apostle Paul, in his famous passage on love in 1 Corinthians 13, describes the qualities of love that reflect God's character: "Love is patient, love is kind. It does not envy, it does not boast, it is not proud. It does not dishonor others, it is not self-seeking, it is not easily angered, it keeps no record of wrongs. Love does not delight in evil but rejoices with the truth. It always protects, always trusts, always hopes, always perseveres" (1 Corinthians 13:4-7). These qualities of love are not just a description of human affection; they are a reflection of the very nature of God.

In a relationship that seeks to reflect God's glory, love must be the guiding principle. This love is not based on feelings or emotions but is a deliberate choice to put the needs of the other person above our own. It is a love that is willing to sacrifice, to forgive, and to serve. When we love our partner in this way, we are not only reflecting the love of God but also inviting others to see His glory in our relationship.

3. The Importance of Grace and Forgiveness in Reflecting God's Glory

Grace and forgiveness are essential components of any relationship that seeks to reflect God's glory. In a fallen world, where sin and brokenness are a reality, there will inevitably be times when we hurt or disappoint each other. In these moments, the way we respond can either reflect the grace and forgiveness of God or contribute to further division and pain.

The grace of God is His unmerited favor toward us—His willingness to forgive our sins and restore our relationship with Him, even though we do not deserve it. In a loving relationship, when we extend grace to our partner, we are reflecting the grace of God. This means being willing to forgive, even when we have been wronged, and to seek reconciliation and healing.

Forgiveness is also a powerful reflection of God's glory. In Matthew 18:21-22, Peter asks Jesus how many times he should forgive his brother or sister who sins against him, and Jesus responds, "I tell you, not seven times, but seventy-seven times." This response highlights the limitless nature of forgiveness that God extends to us, and that we are called to extend to others.

When we forgive our partner, we are not only reflecting the forgiveness of God but also demonstrating the power of His grace to bring healing and restoration. This forgiveness is not always easy, but it is essential for maintaining a healthy and God-glorifying relationship. By forgiving and seeking reconciliation, we are allowing God's glory to be seen in our relationship, and we are inviting others to experience His grace for themselves.

4. The Role of Sacrifice and Service in Reflecting God's Glory

Sacrifice and service are key aspects of a relationship that reflects God's glory. Jesus Himself modeled this kind of sacrificial love when He laid down His life for us. In John 15:13, Jesus says, "Greater love has no one than this: to lay down one's life for one's friends." This sacrificial love is the ultimate reflection of God's glory, and it is the kind of love that we are called to emulate in our relationships.

In a loving relationship, sacrifice means putting the needs and well-being of our partner above our own. It means being willing to give up our own desires, preferences, and comfort for the sake of the other person. This kind of sacrificial love is a powerful reflection of God's love, and it serves as a testament to His goodness and grace.

Service is also an essential aspect of reflecting God's glory in a relationship. Jesus modeled servant leadership when He washed His disciples' feet, demonstrating that true greatness is found in serving others. In a relationship, service means being willing to serve our partner, to meet their needs, and to care for them in practical ways. This service is not about seeking recognition or reward but is an expression of love and a reflection of God's servant-hearted nature.

When we serve and sacrifice for our partner, we are not only reflecting the love of God but also inviting others to see His glory in our relationship. Our acts of service and sacrifice become a powerful witness to the world of the transformative power of God's love.

5. The Impact of Humility in Reflecting God's Glory

Humility is another important quality that reflects God's glory in a relationship. Humility involves recognizing our own limitations and weaknesses and being willing to put the needs of others above our own. It is the opposite of pride, which seeks to exalt oneself and prioritize one's own desires.

In Philippians 2:3-4, Paul writes, "Do nothing out of selfish ambition or vain conceit. Rather, in humility value others above yourselves, not looking to your own interests but each of you to the interests of the others." This passage highlights the importance of humility in our relationships and the way it reflects the character of God.

In a loving relationship, humility means being willing to admit when we are wrong, to seek forgiveness, and to prioritize the needs of our partner. It means being willing to listen, to learn, and to grow together. Humility also involves recognizing that we are not the center of the relationship, but that God is, and that our primary goal is to honor and glorify Him in all that we do.

When we live with humility in our relationships, we are reflecting the humility of Christ, who, though He was in the form of God, did not consider equality with God something to be grasped but made Himself nothing, taking the form of a servant (Philippians 2:6-7). This humility is a powerful reflection of God's glory, and it serves as a testimony to His grace and goodness.

The Role of Prayer and Spiritual Practices in Reflecting God's Glory

Prayer and other spiritual practices play a vital role in reflecting God's glory in a relationship. These practices are not just individual acts of devotion but are also powerful ways to invite God's presence and power into the relationship, allowing His glory to shine through.

1. The Power of Prayer in Reflecting God's Glory

Prayer is one of the most important ways that we can reflect God's glory in our relationships. When we pray together as a couple, we are acknowledging our dependence on God and inviting Him to be the center of our relationship. Prayer helps to align our hearts and minds with God's will, and it opens the door for His power and grace to work in and through us.

In Matthew 18:20, Jesus says, "For where two or three gather in my name, there am I with them." This promise reminds us that God is present in our relationships, especially when we seek Him together in prayer. When we pray together, we are not only drawing closer to each other but also reflecting the glory of God to the world.

Prayer also plays a crucial role in helping us to reflect God's character in our relationships. Through prayer, we can seek God's guidance, wisdom, and strength to love and serve our partner in a way that honors Him. Prayer also helps us to cultivate the qualities of love, grace, humility, and forgiveness that are essential for reflecting God's glory.

2. The Role of Worship in Reflecting God's Glory

Worship is another important spiritual practice that reflects God's glory in a relationship. Worship is not just about singing songs or attending church services; it is about living a life that honors and glorifies God in everything we do. In the context of a relationship, worship involves acknowledging God as the center and foundation of the relationship and seeking to honor Him in all aspects of the relationship.

Worship can take many forms in a relationship, including praying together, reading Scripture together, serving together, and living out the principles of love, grace, and forgiveness. When we make worship a central part of our relationship, we are inviting God's presence and power into the relationship, allowing His glory to shine through.

Worship also involves giving thanks to God for His blessings and grace in our relationship. When we express gratitude to God for our partner and for the love we share, we are acknowledging His goodness and reflecting His glory. This attitude of gratitude can transform our relationship, making it a powerful testimony to the world of God's grace and goodness.

3. The Impact of Studying God's Word Together

Studying God's Word together is another important way to reflect God's glory in a relationship. The Bible is the inspired Word of God, and it is through Scripture that we come to know God more deeply and understand His will for our lives. When we study God's Word together, we are not only growing in our knowledge of God but also allowing His truth to shape and transform our relationship.

Studying Scripture together helps to align our hearts and minds with God's will, and it provides a foundation for making decisions that honor Him. It also helps us to cultivate the qualities of love, grace, humility, and forgiveness that are essential for reflecting God's glory in our relationship.

In addition to studying Scripture together, it is also important to meditate on God's Word and to apply its truths to our relationship. This involves taking time to reflect on what God is saying to us through His Word and seeking to live out those truths in our daily lives. When we do this, we are allowing God's Word to shape and transform our relationship, making it a powerful testimony to His glory.

4. The Importance of Community in Reflecting God's Glory

Finally, community plays an important role in reflecting God's glory in a relationship. As believers, we are called to live in community with other believers, supporting and encouraging one another in our walk with Christ. In the context of a relationship, being part of a community of believers can provide valuable support, accountability, and encouragement.

When we live in community with other believers, we are not only reflecting God's glory in our own relationship but also contributing to the larger body of Christ. Our relationship becomes part of a larger tapestry of God's work in the world, and we are able to encourage and support others in their relationships as well.

Community also provides opportunities to serve together and to reflect God's glory in the way we love and care for others. When we serve others together as a couple, we are reflecting the love and grace of God, and we are making a powerful testimony to His goodness and glory.

The Challenges of Reflecting God's Glory in

Relationships

While reflecting God's glory in a relationship is a beautiful and powerful calling, it is not without its challenges. In a fallen world, where sin and brokenness are a reality, it can be difficult to live out the principles of love, grace, humility, and forgiveness consistently. However, with God's help, it is possible to overcome these challenges and to reflect His glory in our relationships.

1. The Challenge of Sin and Selfishness

One of the biggest challenges to reflecting God's glory in a relationship is the reality of sin and selfishness. As human beings, we are all prone to selfishness, pride, and a desire to put our own needs and desires above those of others. This can create conflict and division in a relationship, making it difficult to reflect the love and grace of God.

The key to overcoming this challenge is to recognize our own sinfulness and to seek God's help in overcoming it. This involves being willing to admit when we are wrong, to seek forgiveness, and to ask God for the grace and strength to live out the principles of love, grace, and humility in our relationship.

It also involves being willing to extend grace and forgiveness to our partner when they fall short. None of us is perfect, and there will be times when we hurt or disappoint each other. In these moments, the way we respond can either reflect the grace and forgiveness of God or contribute to further division and pain.

2. The Challenge of External Pressures

Another challenge to reflecting God's glory in a relationship is the reality of external pressures. In a world that is often hostile to the values and principles of the Christian faith, it can be difficult to live out a relationship that reflects God's glory. External pressures such as work, finances, family, and societal expectations can create stress and tension in a relationship, making it difficult to prioritize and maintain a focus on God.

The key to overcoming this challenge is to keep God at the center of the relationship and to seek His guidance and strength in the face of external pressures. This involves making time for prayer, worship, and studying God's Word together, even when life is busy and stressful. It also involves being intentional about setting priorities and boundaries that honor God and reflect His glory.

Another important aspect of overcoming external pressures is seeking support from a community of believers. Being part of a community of believers can provide valuable support, encouragement, and accountability, helping couples to stay focused on God and to reflect His glory in their relationship.

3. The Challenge of Maintaining Consistency

Maintaining consistency in reflecting God's glory in a relationship can also be a challenge. It is easy to reflect God's glory when things are going well, but it can be more difficult when challenges and difficulties arise. In these moments, it can be tempting to give in to negative emotions such as anger, frustration, or bitterness, rather than reflecting the love and grace of God.

The key to maintaining consistency is to stay rooted in God's love and grace and to seek His strength and guidance in all circumstances. This involves being intentional about cultivating the qualities of love, grace, humility, and forgiveness in our relationship and being willing to seek God's help when we fall short.

It also involves being willing to extend grace and forgiveness to ourselves when we fall short. None of us is perfect, and there will be times when we fail to reflect God's glory in our relationship. In these moments, it is important to seek God's forgiveness and to ask for His help in moving forward and reflecting His glory more consistently.

The Rewards of Reflecting God's Glory in Relationships

While reflecting God's glory in a relationship can be challenging, it also comes with great rewards. When a relationship reflects God's glory, it becomes a powerful testimony to the world of His love, grace, and goodness. It also brings deep joy, fulfillment, and purpose to the couple and to those around them.

1. The Reward of Deepened Intimacy with God and Each Other

One of the greatest rewards of reflecting God's glory in a relationship is the deepened intimacy it brings with God and with each other. When a couple seeks to honor and glorify God in their relationship, they are drawing closer to

Him and to each other. This deepened intimacy creates a strong foundation for a healthy and enduring relationship.

Intimacy with God also brings a sense of peace, joy, and fulfillment that cannot be found in anything else. When a couple is rooted in God's love and grace, they are able to experience the fullness of life in Him, and their relationship becomes a powerful testimony to the world of His goodness and glory.

2. The Reward of Spiritual Growth and Maturity

Reflecting God's glory in a relationship also fosters spiritual growth and maturity, both individually and as a couple. When a couple seeks to live out the principles of love, grace, humility, and forgiveness in their relationship, they are growing in their faith and becoming more like Christ.

This spiritual growth and maturity bring a sense of purpose and meaning to the relationship, as the couple seeks to honor and glorify God in all that they do. It also creates a foundation for a strong and enduring relationship, as the couple grows together in their relationship with God.

3. The Reward of Being a Witness to the World

Finally, reflecting God's glory in a relationship creates a powerful witness to the world of His love, grace, and goodness. In a world that is often darkened by selfishness, division, and hatred, a relationship that reflects God's glory stands out as a beacon of light, pointing others to the reality of God's love and grace.

This witness is not just about words or actions but is about living a life that reflects the character of God. When a couple seeks to honor and glorify God in their relationship, they are inviting others to experience His love and grace for themselves. This witness can have a profound impact on those around them, leading others to a deeper understanding of God's love and to a relationship with Him.

Conclusion

Reflecting God's glory in a relationship is a beautiful and powerful calling. It is about living in such a way that others can see the character of God in us and through us be drawn to worship and glorify Him. This reflection of God's glory is not just for our own benefit but is a powerful testimony to the world of His love, grace, and goodness.

As we reflect on the words of Matthew 5:16, "Let your light shine before others, that they may see your good deeds and glorify your Father in heaven," let us be reminded of the importance of reflecting God's glory in our relationships. May we always seek to live out the principles of love, grace, humility, and forgiveness, and to honor and glorify God in all that we do. And may our relationships become a powerful testimony to the world of God's love and grace, as we walk in faith, trust, and love, with Christ as our guide.

Chapter 13: Overcoming Fear with Perfect Love

Introduction

Fear is one of the most powerful and pervasive emotions that humans experience. It has the potential to paralyze us, to inhibit our ability to love freely, and to create barriers in our relationships. In the context of a loving relationship, fear can manifest in various forms—fear of vulnerability, fear of rejection, fear of loss, or fear of the unknown. However, the Bible provides a profound truth that offers hope and freedom: "There is no fear in love, but perfect love casts out fear" (1 John 4:18). This chapter explores how love, particularly the assurance of God's perfect love, can overcome fear and bring healing and freedom to our relationships.

Understanding the Nature of Fear in Relationships

Fear, at its core, is a response to perceived danger or threat. It is a natural emotion that has evolved to protect us from harm, but in relationships, fear often stems from deeper emotional and psychological concerns. In relationships, fear can arise from past experiences, insecurities, or the uncertainties of the future. It can manifest as fear of vulnerability, fear of rejection, fear of loss, or fear of abandonment. These fears can create barriers that prevent us from fully experiencing and expressing love.

1. The Fear of Vulnerability

One of the most common fears in relationships is the fear of vulnerability. To be vulnerable means to open ourselves up to another person, to share our deepest thoughts, feelings, and fears, and to risk being hurt. This fear often stems from past experiences of betrayal, rejection, or disappointment. When we have been hurt in the past, it can be difficult to trust again, and we may build walls around our hearts to protect ourselves.

However, vulnerability is essential for deep, meaningful relationships. It is through vulnerability that we connect with others on a deeper level, that we experience intimacy and trust, and that we allow love to flourish. The fear of vulnerability can prevent us from experiencing the fullness of love and can create distance in our relationships.

2. The Fear of Rejection

The fear of rejection is another common fear in relationships. This fear often stems from a deep-seated need for acceptance and belonging. When we fear rejection, we may hold back parts of ourselves, hide our true feelings, or avoid taking risks in the relationship. This fear can prevent us from fully committing to the relationship or from expressing our love and affection freely.

The fear of rejection can also lead to behaviors that undermine the relationship, such as people-pleasing, seeking constant reassurance, or avoiding conflict. These behaviors can create a sense of insecurity in the relationship and prevent both partners from experiencing the depth of love that is possible.

3. The Fear of Loss

The fear of loss is another significant fear that can affect relationships. This fear can manifest as a fear of losing the relationship itself, a fear of losing the other person, or a fear of losing one's sense of self within the relationship. The fear of loss can create anxiety, clinginess, or possessiveness in the relationship, which can ultimately drive the other person away.

The fear of loss can also prevent us from fully enjoying the relationship in the present moment. When we are constantly worried about the future or about what might happen, we may miss out on the joy and beauty of the relationship as it is now. This fear can create a sense of insecurity and unease in the relationship, which can undermine trust and intimacy.

4. The Fear of the Unknown

The fear of the unknown is another fear that can affect relationships. This fear often arises from uncertainties about the future, about the direction of the relationship, or about changes that may occur. The fear of the unknown can create anxiety and stress in the relationship, as we may worry about what might happen or about things that are beyond our control.

The fear of the unknown can also prevent us from taking risks in the relationship or from embracing change. It can create a sense of stagnation or complacency in the relationship, as we may resist growth or change out of fear of the unknown. This fear can prevent the relationship from evolving and deepening over time.

The Power of God's Perfect Love

The good news is that there is a powerful antidote to fear, and that is love—specifically, God's perfect love. The Bible tells us that "there is no fear in love, but perfect love casts out fear" (1 John 4:18). This verse offers a profound truth: God's perfect love has the power to overcome fear, to bring healing and freedom, and to enable us to love more fully and freely.

1. Understanding God's Perfect Love

To understand how God's perfect love can overcome fear, we must first understand what it means for love to be "perfect." In this context, "perfect" does not mean flawless or without error. Instead, it refers to love that is complete, mature, and fully realized. God's love is perfect because it is whole, lacking nothing, and because it is rooted in His unchanging character.

God's love is perfect in several ways:

- Unconditional Love: God's love is unconditional, meaning that it is not based on our performance, our worthiness, or our ability to earn it. God's love is given freely, regardless of our flaws, failures, or shortcomings. This unconditional love provides a foundation of security and acceptance, which can overcome the fear of rejection.

- Sacrificial Love: God's love is sacrificial, as demonstrated by the ultimate act of love—Jesus Christ laying down His life for us. This sacrificial love shows us that God's love is not just a feeling or an emotion but an action, a commitment to our well-being and salvation. This sacrificial love provides assurance and confidence, which can overcome the fear of loss.

- Faithful Love: God's love is faithful and steadfast. He is always with us, He never abandons us, and His love never changes. This faithfulness provides a sense of stability and trust, which can overcome the fear of the unknown.

- Perfecting Love: God's love is also a perfecting love, meaning that it is actively at work in our lives to transform us, to heal us, and to make us more like Christ. This perfecting love provides hope and encouragement, which can overcome the fear of vulnerability.

2. How God's Perfect Love Casts Out Fear

When we experience and embrace God's perfect love, it has the power to cast out fear in our lives and in our relationships. This is not just a one-time event but an ongoing process of allowing God's love to penetrate our hearts and to transform our fears into faith, trust, and confidence.

- Casting Out the Fear of Vulnerability: When we know that we are fully loved and accepted by God, we no longer need to fear being vulnerable with others. God's perfect love gives us the courage to open our hearts, to share our true selves, and to take the risk of being known and loved. This vulnerability is essential for deep, meaningful relationships, and it allows love to flourish.

- Casting Out the Fear of Rejection: When we are rooted in the security of God's unconditional love, we no longer need to fear rejection. We know that our worth and value are not determined by others' acceptance or approval but by God's love for us. This confidence allows us to love freely, without fear of rejection, and to build relationships based on mutual respect and trust.

- Casting Out the Fear of Loss: When we trust in God's sacrificial love, we no longer need to fear loss. We know that God is in control, that He is working all things for our good, and that His love for us is eternal. This assurance gives us the freedom to love fully in the present, without clinging or possessiveness, and to trust God with the future.

- Casting Out the Fear of the Unknown: When we rest in God's faithful love, we no longer need to fear the unknown. We know that God is with us, that He will never leave us, and that He is guiding our steps. This trust allows us to embrace change, to take risks, and to move forward in faith, knowing that God is leading us.

Applying God's Perfect Love in Relationships

While understanding the power of God's perfect love is important, it is equally important to know how to apply this love in our relationships. The following sections will explore practical ways to allow God's perfect love to cast out fear and to bring healing and freedom to our relationships.

1. Embracing Vulnerability with Confidence in God's Love

One of the most powerful ways to overcome the fear of vulnerability is to embrace it with confidence in God's love. Vulnerability is not a weakness but a strength, as it allows us to connect with others on a deeper level and to experience true intimacy.

To embrace vulnerability in a relationship, it is important to:

- Acknowledge the Fear: The first step in overcoming the fear of vulnerability is to acknowledge it. Recognize the ways in which fear may be holding you back from fully opening up to your partner and from allowing yourself to be known and loved.

- Root Yourself in God's Love: Remind yourself of God's unconditional love for you. Spend time in prayer and meditation, reflecting on the truth that you are fully loved and accepted by God, just as you are. This security in God's love gives you the confidence to be vulnerable with others.

- Take Small Steps: Start by taking small steps toward vulnerability in your relationship. Share something personal with your partner, express your feelings, or ask for support. As you take these steps, you will build trust and intimacy in your relationship.

- Seek Support: If the fear of vulnerability is particularly strong, consider seeking support from a counselor, therapist, or trusted spiritual mentor. They can help you work through the fear and develop the confidence to embrace vulnerability in your relationship.

2. Building Trust and Overcoming the Fear of Rejection

Trust is the foundation of any healthy relationship, and it is essential for overcoming the fear of rejection. Building trust takes time, effort, and intentionality, but it is worth the investment.

To build trust and overcome the fear of rejection in a relationship, consider the following:

- Communicate Openly and Honestly: Trust is built through open and honest communication. Be willing to share your thoughts, feelings, and concerns with your partner, and be open to hearing theirs. This communication fosters transparency and builds trust.

- Show Consistency and Reliability: Trust is also built through consistency and reliability. Be dependable in your actions and words, and show your partner that they can count on you. This reliability helps to create a sense of security in the relationship.

- Extend Grace and Forgiveness: Trust is not just about avoiding mistakes but about how we handle them when they happen. When trust is broken, it is important to extend grace and forgiveness to one another. This forgiveness allows the relationship to heal and to grow stronger.

- Affirm Each Other's Value: Regularly affirm your partner's value and worth in the relationship. Let them know that they are loved, accepted, and appreciated. This affirmation helps to counteract the fear of rejection and builds confidence in the relationship.

3. Cultivating a Secure Attachment and Overcoming the Fear of Loss

The fear of loss can create anxiety and insecurity in a relationship, but cultivating a secure attachment can help to overcome this fear. A secure attachment is characterized by a sense of safety, trust, and stability in the relationship.

To cultivate a secure attachment and overcome the fear of loss, consider the following:

- Prioritize Emotional Connection: A secure attachment is built on a strong emotional connection. Make time to connect with your partner on an emotional level, through shared experiences, meaningful conversations, and expressions of affection.

- Be Present and Attentive: Show your partner that you are present and attentive in the relationship. This presence reassures them of your commitment and helps to create a sense of security.

- Manage Conflict Constructively: Conflict is a natural part of any relationship, but how it is managed can impact the sense of security in the relationship. Approach conflict with a spirit of love, respect, and a desire for resolution. This constructive approach helps to maintain a secure attachment.

- Trust in God's Sovereignty: Ultimately, overcoming the fear of loss requires trusting in God's sovereignty. Trust that God is in control of your relationship and that He is working all things for your good. This trust allows you to release the fear of loss and to embrace the relationship with confidence.

4. Embracing Change and Overcoming the Fear of the Unknown

The fear of the unknown can create anxiety and stress in a relationship, but embracing change with faith and trust in God can help to overcome this fear. Change is a natural part of life and relationships, and it can bring growth and new opportunities.

To embrace change and overcome the fear of the unknown, consider the following:

- Focus on the Present: While it is natural to think about the future, it is important to focus on the present moment. Enjoy the relationship as it is now, and trust that God will guide you through whatever changes or challenges may come.

- Embrace a Growth Mindset: View change as an opportunity for growth, both individually and as a couple. Embrace the challenges and opportunities that come with change, and trust that God is using them to strengthen your relationship.

- Seek God's Guidance: When facing the unknown, seek God's guidance through prayer, Scripture, and the counsel of trusted spiritual mentors. Trust that God is leading you and that He has a plan for your relationship.

- Support Each Other: Change can be challenging, but facing it together with love and support can strengthen your relationship. Be there for each other, offer encouragement, and work together to navigate the changes that come your way.

The Transformative Power of Love in Relationships

When fear is cast out by God's perfect love, it transforms relationships in powerful ways. It allows love to flourish, trust to deepen, and intimacy to grow. It also creates a foundation of security, confidence, and peace, which enables the relationship to thrive.

1. Love that Fosters Intimacy and Connection

When fear is cast out by God's perfect love, it creates an environment where intimacy and connection can flourish. Without the barriers of fear, couples can open their hearts to one another, share their deepest thoughts and feelings, and experience true intimacy. This intimacy is not just physical but emotional and spiritual as well.

Intimacy and connection are essential for a healthy and fulfilling relationship. They create a sense of closeness and bonding that strengthens the relationship and allows it to withstand challenges. When love casts out fear, it allows couples to experience the fullness of intimacy and connection that God intended for relationships.

2. Love that Builds Trust and Security

When fear is cast out by God's perfect love, it builds trust and security in the relationship. Without the fear of rejection, loss, or the unknown, couples can trust one another more deeply and feel secure in the relationship. This trust and security create a strong foundation for the relationship and allow it to grow and thrive.

Trust and security are essential for a healthy relationship. They create a sense of safety and stability that allows couples to navigate challenges and uncertainties with confidence. When love casts out fear, it allows couples to experience the trust and security that are necessary for a lasting and fulfilling relationship.

3. Love that Encourages Growth and Transformation

When fear is cast out by God's perfect love, it encourages growth and transformation in the relationship. Without the fear of vulnerability or the unknown, couples can embrace change, take risks, and grow together. This growth and transformation allow the relationship to evolve and deepen over time.

Growth and transformation are essential for a healthy relationship. They allow couples to adapt to changes, to learn from challenges, and to become more like Christ in their love for one another. When love casts out fear, it allows couples to experience the growth and transformation that are necessary for a vibrant and fulfilling relationship.

4. Love that Reflects God's Glory

When fear is cast out by God's perfect love, it allows the relationship to reflect God's glory to the world. Without the barriers of fear, couples can live out the principles of love, grace, forgiveness, and humility in their relationship. This reflection of God's love and character serves as a powerful testimony to the world of His goodness and grace.

Reflecting God's glory is the ultimate purpose of any relationship. It is about living in such a way that others can see the character of God in us and through us be drawn to worship and glorify Him. When love casts out fear, it allows couples to experience the fullness of God's love and to reflect His glory in their relationship.

The Rewards of Overcoming Fear with Perfect Love

While overcoming fear with perfect love can be challenging, it also comes with great rewards. When fear is cast out by God's perfect love, it brings healing, freedom, and joy to the relationship. It also creates a foundation of trust, intimacy, and security that allows the relationship to thrive.

1. The Reward of Healing and Freedom

One of the greatest rewards of overcoming fear with perfect love is the healing and freedom that it brings to the relationship. When fear is cast out by God's love, it brings healing to past wounds, insecurities, and hurts. It also brings freedom from the chains of fear, allowing couples to experience the fullness of love and to live without fear.

Healing and freedom are essential for a healthy relationship. They allow couples to move forward without the baggage of the past, to trust one another more deeply, and to experience the joy and beauty of the relationship. When love casts out fear, it allows couples to experience the healing and freedom that are necessary for a fulfilling relationship.

2. The Reward of Deepened Love and Intimacy

Another reward of overcoming fear with perfect love is the deepened love and intimacy that it brings to the relationship. When fear is cast out by God's love, it creates an environment where love can flourish, trust can deepen, and intimacy can grow. This deepened love and intimacy create a strong foundation for the relationship and allow it to withstand challenges.

Deepened love and intimacy are essential for a healthy relationship. They create a sense of closeness and bonding that strengthens the relationship and allows it to thrive. When love casts out fear, it allows couples to experience the deepened love and intimacy that are necessary for a lasting and fulfilling relationship.

3. The Reward of Security and Peace

Overcoming fear with perfect love also brings the reward of security and peace to the relationship. When fear is cast out by God's love, it creates a sense of safety and stability in the relationship. This security and peace allow couples to navigate challenges and uncertainties with confidence and trust in God's sovereignty.

Security and peace are essential for a healthy relationship. They create a foundation of stability that allows couples to build a life together and to face the future with confidence. When love casts out fear, it allows couples to experience the security and peace that are necessary for a fulfilling relationship.

4. The Reward of Reflecting God's Glory

Finally, overcoming fear with perfect love brings the reward of reflecting God's glory in the relationship. When fear is cast out by God's love, it allows the relationship to reflect the character of God to the world. This reflection of God's love and character serves as a powerful testimony to the world of His goodness and grace.

Reflecting God's glory is the ultimate purpose of any relationship. It is about living in such a way that others can see the character of God in us and through us be drawn to worship and glorify Him. When love casts out fear, it allows couples to experience the fullness of God's love and to reflect His glory in their relationship.

Conclusion

Fear is a powerful emotion that can create barriers in relationships and prevent us from fully experiencing and expressing love. However, the Bible offers a profound truth: "There is no fear in love, but perfect love casts out fear" (1 John 4:18). God's perfect love has the power to overcome fear, to bring healing and freedom, and to enable us to love more fully and freely.

As we reflect on the power of God's perfect love, let us be reminded of the importance of allowing His love to cast out fear in our relationships. May we always seek to root ourselves in God's love, to build trust and intimacy in our relationships, and to reflect His glory in all that we do. And may we experience the fullness of love and life together, as we walk in faith, trust, and love, with Christ as our guide.

Chapter 14: Unity in Love: Becoming One

Introduction

Unity is a powerful and essential aspect of love, especially in the context of a marriage or committed relationship. It is through unity that two individuals come together, not only in body but in spirit and purpose, to create a bond that reflects the divine relationship between Christ and the Church. The Bible teaches us in Genesis 2:24 that "Therefore a man shall leave his father and his mother and hold fast to his wife, and they shall become one flesh." This verse encapsulates the profound mystery of two becoming one—a unity that is both spiritual and emotional, built on love and sustained by faith. This chapter explores the concept of unity in love, examining how a loving relationship can achieve spiritual and emotional unity, becoming one in purpose and spirit, with faith as the cornerstone of this unity.

The Biblical Foundation of Unity in Love

The concept of unity in love is deeply rooted in Scripture, beginning with the creation narrative in Genesis. The idea of two becoming one is not just a physical union but a profound spiritual and emotional connection that reflects the nature of God's relationship with His people. This unity is foundational to a healthy and fulfilling relationship, and it serves as a testament to God's design for love and marriage.

1. The Genesis Narrative: A Blueprint for Unity

The foundation of unity in love is laid in the creation narrative in Genesis. In Genesis 2:18, God declares, "It is not good that the man should be alone; I will make him a helper fit for him." This statement highlights the importance of companionship and unity in God's design for humanity. God created Eve as a companion for Adam, someone who would complement him and with whom he could form a unified partnership.

Genesis 2:24 further emphasizes this unity: "Therefore a man shall leave his father and his mother and hold fast to his wife, and they shall become one flesh." This verse is often quoted in the context of marriage, but its implications go far beyond the physical union of a husband and wife. The phrase "one flesh" signifies a profound unity that encompasses every aspect of the relationship—physical, emotional, spiritual, and relational.

The unity described in Genesis is not just about living together or sharing a life; it is about becoming one in purpose, spirit, and identity. This unity reflects the unity within the Trinity—Father, Son, and Holy Spirit—three distinct persons, yet one in essence and purpose. In the same way, a loving relationship that achieves unity reflects the divine relationship between God and His people.

2. The New Testament Affirmation of Unity

The New Testament continues to affirm the importance of unity in love, particularly in the context of marriage. Jesus Himself refers to Genesis 2:24 when teaching about marriage, emphasizing that what God has joined together, no one should separate (Matthew 19:6). This underscores the permanence and sacredness of the unity in marriage, as well as the idea that it is divinely ordained.

The Apostle Paul also speaks extensively about unity in his letters, particularly in the context of the relationship between Christ and the Church. In Ephesians 5:31-32, Paul quotes Genesis 2:24 and then explains, "This is a profound mystery—but I am talking about Christ and the church." Here, Paul reveals that the unity between a husband and wife is a reflection of the unity between Christ and the Church. Just as Christ and the Church are one, so too are husband and wife called to become one in love, purpose, and spirit.

Paul also speaks of the unity of believers in the body of Christ, emphasizing that we are all members of one body, united in Christ (1 Corinthians 12:12-13). This unity in the body of Christ serves as a model for the unity that should exist in a loving relationship—a unity that is characterized by mutual love, respect, and a shared commitment to God's purpose.

The Spiritual Aspect of Unity in Love

While unity in love certainly includes physical and emotional aspects, it is ultimately rooted in the spiritual connection between two individuals. This spiritual unity is what allows a relationship to transcend the challenges and trials of life and to reflect the love and grace of God.

1. Unity in Spirit: A Shared Faith

The foundation of spiritual unity in a relationship is a shared faith in God. When both partners are committed to following Christ and living according to His teachings, their relationship is built on a solid foundation that can withstand the challenges of life. This shared faith creates a bond that goes beyond the physical and emotional connection, anchoring the relationship in something eternal and unchanging.

A shared faith also provides a common purpose and direction for the relationship. When both partners are committed to serving God and following His will, they are united in their goals and aspirations. This unity of purpose helps to align their priorities and decisions, making it easier to navigate the challenges of life together.

In addition, a shared faith allows for spiritual intimacy in the relationship. This intimacy is cultivated through shared spiritual practices, such as prayer, worship, and studying God's Word together. When both partners are growing in their relationship with God, they are also growing closer to each other, creating a deep and lasting spiritual bond.

2. The Role of the Holy Spirit in Unity

The Holy Spirit plays a crucial role in creating and sustaining spiritual unity in a relationship. The Holy Spirit is the source of the love, grace, and wisdom that are necessary for a relationship to thrive. When both partners are open to the leading of the Holy Spirit, they are able to experience a unity that goes beyond human effort or understanding.

The Holy Spirit also empowers believers to live out the principles of love, grace, and forgiveness that are essential for unity. In Galatians 5:22-23, Paul lists the fruit of the Spirit, which includes love, joy, peace, patience, kindness, goodness, faithfulness, gentleness, and self-control. These qualities are the building blocks of unity in a relationship, and they are produced in our lives through the work of the Holy Spirit.

In addition, the Holy Spirit helps to guide and direct the relationship according to God's will. When both partners are seeking the guidance of the Holy Spirit, they are able to make decisions that are in line with God's purpose for their relationship. This alignment with God's will is what creates true unity in the relationship, as both partners are moving in the same direction, guided by the same Spirit.

3. The Power of Prayer in Achieving Spiritual Unity

Prayer is one of the most powerful tools for achieving and maintaining spiritual unity in a relationship. When couples pray together, they are inviting God into their relationship and seeking His guidance, wisdom, and blessing. Prayer creates a space for both partners to connect with God and with each other on a deeper level, fostering spiritual intimacy and unity.

Praying together also helps to align the hearts and minds of both partners with God's will. When couples seek God's guidance in prayer, they are more likely to make decisions that are in line with His purpose for their relationship. This alignment with God's will helps to create unity in the relationship, as both partners are moving in the same direction, guided by the same Spirit.

In addition, prayer helps to cultivate the qualities of love, grace, and forgiveness that are essential for unity. When couples pray for each other, they are more likely to extend grace and forgiveness, to be patient and understanding, and to seek the best for each other. This creates a strong foundation for unity in the relationship, as both partners are committed to loving and serving each other in a Christ-like manner.

The Emotional Aspect of Unity in Love

While spiritual unity is the foundation of a loving relationship, emotional unity is also essential for a relationship to thrive. Emotional unity involves a deep connection between two individuals, characterized by mutual love, trust, and understanding. This emotional connection is what allows a relationship to withstand the challenges of life and to grow deeper over time.

1. The Importance of Emotional Intimacy

Emotional intimacy is the key to achieving emotional unity in a relationship. Emotional intimacy involves being open and vulnerable with each other, sharing your thoughts, feelings, and experiences, and being willing to listen and understand each other. This openness and vulnerability create a deep emotional connection that strengthens the bond between partners.

Emotional intimacy also involves being supportive and caring for each other. This means being there for each other in times of need, offering comfort and encouragement, and showing love and affection. This support and care create a sense of security and trust in the relationship, which is essential for emotional unity.

In addition, emotional intimacy involves being willing to work through conflicts and challenges together. No relationship is without its difficulties, but emotional unity allows couples to face these challenges together, to seek resolution and healing, and to grow closer through the process.

2. Building Trust in Emotional Unity

Trust is the foundation of emotional unity in a relationship. Without trust, it is difficult to achieve true emotional intimacy and connection. Trust involves being reliable and dependable, keeping your promises, and being honest and transparent with each other.

Building trust in a relationship takes time and effort, but it is essential for emotional unity. Trust is built through consistent actions and behaviors that demonstrate your love and commitment to your partner. This includes being there for each other in times of need, being honest and open in your communication, and being willing to forgive and seek reconciliation when trust is broken.

Trust also involves being willing to take risks in the relationship, to be vulnerable and open with each other, and to trust that your partner will respond with love and care. This willingness to take risks and to trust each other is what creates emotional unity in the relationship, as both partners are able to connect on a deeper level and to build a strong emotional bond.

3. The Role of Communication in Emotional Unity

Communication is another essential component of emotional unity in a relationship. Communication involves more than just talking to each other; it involves listening, understanding, and empathizing with each other. Effective communication allows couples to connect on an emotional level, to share their thoughts and feelings, and to work through conflicts and challenges together.

Effective communication involves being open and honest with each other, being willing to listen and understand each other's perspectives, and being respectful and kind in your communication. It also involves being willing to address conflicts and challenges in a constructive manner, seeking resolution and healing rather than allowing issues to fester and create division.

Communication is also essential for maintaining emotional unity over time. As couples grow and change, their needs and desires may also change, and effective communication allows couples to stay connected and to continue to build emotional unity in their relationship.

4. The Role of Forgiveness in Emotional Unity

Forgiveness is another key component of emotional unity in a relationship. No relationship is without its challenges and conflicts, and there will be times when both partners hurt or disappoint each other. In these moments, the ability to forgive and seek reconciliation is essential for maintaining emotional unity in the relationship.

Forgiveness involves letting go of resentment and anger, seeking to understand and empathize with the other person, and being willing to extend grace and mercy. It also involves being willing to seek forgiveness when you have hurt or wronged your partner, and to work together to rebuild trust and unity in the relationship.

Forgiveness is not always easy, but it is essential for emotional unity in a relationship. When couples are willing to forgive and seek reconciliation, they are able to move past conflicts and challenges and to grow closer through the process. This creates a strong foundation for emotional unity in the relationship, as both partners are committed to loving and supporting each other in a Christ-like manner.

Becoming One in Purpose and Spirit

Achieving unity in love involves more than just emotional and spiritual connection; it also involves becoming one in purpose and spirit. This means aligning your goals, values, and priorities, and working together as a team to achieve them. It also means being committed to a shared vision for your relationship and your life together.

1. Aligning Goals and Priorities

One of the key aspects of becoming one in purpose and spirit is aligning your goals and priorities as a couple. This involves discussing your individual goals and desires, and finding ways to align them with the goals and desires of your partner. This alignment creates a sense of unity and purpose in the relationship, as both partners are working toward the same goals and aspirations.

Aligning your goals and priorities also involves being willing to compromise and to support each other in achieving your individual goals. This means being willing to make sacrifices for the sake of the relationship, and being committed to helping each other achieve your dreams and aspirations.

In addition, aligning your goals and priorities involves being intentional about setting goals and priorities for your relationship. This includes setting goals for your spiritual growth, your emotional connection, your communication, and your relationship as a whole. Being intentional about setting and working toward these goals helps to create a sense of purpose and direction in the relationship, and fosters unity in purpose and spirit.

2. Working Together as a Team

Becoming one in purpose and spirit also involves working together as a team. This means being committed to supporting each other, to working together to overcome challenges, and to achieving your goals and aspirations as a couple.

Working together as a team involves being willing to communicate and collaborate with each other, to share responsibilities and to make decisions together. It also involves being willing to support each other in times of need, to offer encouragement and comfort, and to work together to find solutions to problems.

Working together as a team also involves being willing to put the needs of the relationship above your individual desires. This means being willing to make sacrifices for the sake of the relationship, to prioritize your partner's needs and desires, and to be committed to the success of the relationship as a whole.

3. Being Committed to a Shared Vision

Another key aspect of becoming one in purpose and spirit is being committed to a shared vision for your relationship and your life together. This shared vision is the foundation of your relationship, and it provides direction and purpose for your life together.

A shared vision involves discussing your individual goals and desires, and finding ways to align them with the goals and desires of your partner. It also involves being intentional about setting goals and priorities for your relationship, and being committed to achieving them together.

A shared vision also involves being committed to the success of the relationship, and being willing to make sacrifices for the sake of the relationship. This means being willing to put the needs of the relationship above your individual desires, to prioritize your partner's needs and desires, and to be committed to the success of the relationship as a whole.

4. Being Open to Growth and Change

Becoming one in purpose and spirit also involves being open to growth and change in the relationship. Relationships are not static; they are dynamic and constantly evolving. This means being willing to adapt and to grow together as a couple, to embrace change, and to be open to new experiences and opportunities.

Being open to growth and change also involves being willing to work through challenges and conflicts together, to seek resolution and healing, and to grow closer through the process. It also involves being open to new experiences and opportunities, and being willing to take risks and to step out of your comfort zone.

Being open to growth and change is essential for achieving unity in purpose and spirit, as it allows the relationship to evolve and deepen over time. This openness creates a sense of unity and purpose in the relationship, as both partners are committed to growing and evolving together.

The Role of Faith in Achieving Unity in Love

Faith plays a crucial role in achieving unity in love. It is through faith that we are able to connect with God, to receive His guidance and wisdom, and to experience the love, grace, and forgiveness that are essential for unity in a relationship.

1. Faith as the Foundation of Unity

Faith is the foundation of unity in love. When both partners are committed to following Christ and living according to His teachings, their relationship is built on a solid foundation that can withstand the challenges of life. This shared faith creates a bond that goes beyond the physical and emotional connection, anchoring the relationship in something eternal and unchanging.

Faith also provides a common purpose and direction for the relationship. When both partners are committed to serving God and following His will, they are united in their goals and aspirations. This unity of purpose helps to align their priorities and decisions, making it easier to navigate the challenges of life together.

In addition, faith allows for spiritual intimacy in the relationship. This intimacy is cultivated through shared spiritual practices, such as prayer, worship, and studying God's Word together. When both partners are growing in their relationship with God, they are also growing closer to each other, creating a deep and lasting spiritual bond.

2. The Role of Trust in Faith

Trust is a key component of faith, and it plays a crucial role in achieving unity in love. Trust involves being willing to rely on God, to trust in His plan for your relationship, and to trust that He will provide the guidance, wisdom, and strength needed to navigate the challenges of life.

Trust also involves being willing to trust your partner, to rely on their love and support, and to be vulnerable and open with them. This trust creates a strong foundation for unity in the relationship, as both partners are able to rely on each other and to work together as a team.

In addition, trust involves being willing to take risks in the relationship, to step out in faith, and to be open to new experiences and opportunities. This willingness to take risks and to trust in God's plan is essential for achieving unity in purpose and spirit, as it allows the relationship to grow and evolve over time.

3. The Power of Prayer in Faith

Prayer is one of the most powerful tools for achieving and maintaining unity in love. When couples pray together, they are inviting God into their relationship and seeking His guidance, wisdom, and blessing. Prayer creates a space for both partners to connect with God and with each other on a deeper level, fostering spiritual intimacy and unity.

Praying together also helps to align the hearts and minds of both partners with God's will. When couples seek God's guidance in prayer, they are more likely to make decisions that are in line with His purpose for their relationship. This alignment with God's will helps to create unity in the relationship, as both partners are moving in the same direction, guided by the same Spirit.

In addition, prayer helps to cultivate the qualities of love, grace, and forgiveness that are essential for unity. When couples pray for each other, they are more likely to extend grace and forgiveness, to be patient and understanding, and to seek the best for each other. This creates a strong foundation for unity in the relationship, as both partners are committed to loving and serving each other in a Christ-like manner.

4. The Role of Worship in Faith

Worship is another important spiritual practice that plays a crucial role in achieving unity in love. Worship is not just about singing songs or attending church services; it is about living a life that honors and glorifies God in everything you do. In the context of a relationship, worship involves acknowledging God as the center and foundation of the relationship and seeking to honor Him in all aspects of the relationship.

Worship can take many forms in a relationship, including praying together, reading Scripture together, serving together, and living out the principles of love, grace, and forgiveness. When both partners are committed to worshiping God together, they are united in their purpose and direction, and they are able to build a strong foundation for unity in their relationship.

Worship also involves giving thanks to God for His blessings and grace in your relationship. When couples express gratitude to God for each other and for the love they share, they are acknowledging His goodness and reflecting His glory. This attitude of gratitude can transform your relationship, making it a powerful testimony to the world of God's grace and goodness.

The Challenges of Achieving Unity in Love

While achieving unity in love is a beautiful and powerful calling, it is not without its challenges. In a fallen world, where sin and brokenness are a reality, it can be difficult to achieve and maintain unity in a relationship. However, with God's help, it is possible to overcome these challenges and to achieve true unity in love.

1. The Challenge of Sin and Selfishness

One of the biggest challenges to achieving unity in love is the reality of sin and selfishness. As human beings, we are all prone to selfishness, pride, and a desire to put our own needs and desires above those of others. This can create conflict and division in a relationship, making it difficult to achieve true unity.

The key to overcoming this challenge is to recognize our own sinfulness and to seek God's help in overcoming it. This involves being willing to admit when we are wrong, to seek forgiveness, and to ask God for the grace and strength to live out the principles of love, grace, and humility in our relationship.

It also involves being willing to extend grace and forgiveness to our partner when they fall short. None of us is perfect, and there will be times when we hurt or disappoint each other. In these moments, the way we respond can either reflect the grace and forgiveness of God or contribute to further division and pain.

2. The Challenge of External Pressures

Another challenge to achieving unity in love is the reality of external pressures. In a world that is often hostile to the values and principles of the Christian faith, it can be difficult to live out a relationship that reflects God's glory. External pressures such as work, finances, family, and societal expectations can create stress and tension in a relationship, making it difficult to prioritize and maintain a focus on God.

The key to overcoming this challenge is to keep God at the center of the relationship and to seek His guidance and strength in the face of external pressures. This involves making time for prayer, worship, and studying God's Word together, even when life is busy and stressful. It also involves being intentional about setting priorities and boundaries that honor God and reflect His glory.

Another important aspect of overcoming external pressures is seeking support from a community of believers. Being part of a community of believers can provide valuable support, encouragement, and accountability, helping couples to stay focused on God and to achieve unity in their relationship.

3. The Challenge of Maintaining Consistency

Maintaining consistency in achieving and maintaining unity in love can also be a challenge. It is easy to focus on unity when things are going well, but it can be more difficult when challenges and difficulties arise. In these moments, it can be tempting to give in to negative emotions such as anger, frustration, or bitterness, rather than seeking to maintain unity in the relationship.

The key to maintaining consistency is to stay rooted in God's love and grace and to seek His strength and guidance in all circumstances. This involves being intentional about cultivating the qualities of love, grace, humility, and forgiveness in your relationship, and being willing to seek God's help when you fall short.

It also involves being willing to extend grace and forgiveness to yourself when you fall short. None of us is perfect, and there will be times when we fail to maintain unity in our relationship. In these moments, it is important to seek God's forgiveness and to ask for His help in moving forward and achieving unity in love.

The Rewards of Achieving Unity in Love

While achieving unity in love can be challenging, it also comes with great rewards. When a relationship achieves unity in love, it becomes a powerful testimony to the world of God's love, grace, and goodness. It also brings deep joy, fulfillment, and purpose to the couple and to those around them.

1. The Reward of Deepened Intimacy and Connection

One of the greatest rewards of achieving unity in love is the deepened intimacy and connection that it brings to the relationship. When a couple is united in spirit, purpose, and love, they are able to experience a level of intimacy and connection that goes beyond the physical and emotional. This deepened intimacy creates a strong foundation for a healthy and enduring relationship.

Intimacy with God also brings a sense of peace, joy, and fulfillment that cannot be found in anything else. When a couple is rooted in God's love and grace, they are able to experience the fullness of life in Him, and their relationship becomes a powerful testimony to the world of His goodness and glory.

2. The Reward of Spiritual Growth and Maturity

Achieving unity in love also fosters spiritual growth and maturity, both individually and as a couple. When a couple is united in their commitment to following Christ and living according to His teachings, they are growing in their faith and becoming more like Christ.

This spiritual growth and maturity bring a sense of purpose and meaning to the relationship, as the couple seeks to honor and glorify God in all that they do. It also creates a foundation for a strong and enduring relationship, as the couple grows together in their relationship with God.

3. The Reward of Being a Witness to the World

Finally, achieving unity in love creates a powerful witness to the world of God's love, grace, and goodness. In a world that is often darkened by selfishness, division, and hatred, a relationship that achieves unity in love stands out as a beacon of light, pointing others to the reality of God's love and grace.

This witness is not just about words or actions, but about living a life that reflects the character of God. When a couple is united in their commitment to following Christ and living according to His teachings, they are inviting others to experience His love and grace for themselves. This witness can have a profound impact on those around them, leading others to a deeper understanding of God's love and to a relationship with Him.

Conclusion

Unity in love is a powerful and essential aspect of a loving relationship. It is through unity that two individuals come together, not only in body but in spirit and purpose, to create a bond that reflects the divine relationship between Christ and the Church. The Bible teaches us in Genesis 2:24 that "Therefore a man shall leave his father and his mother and hold fast to his wife, and they shall become one flesh." This verse encapsulates the profound mystery of two becoming one—a unity that is both spiritual and emotional, built on love and sustained by faith.

As we reflect on the concept of unity in love, let us be reminded of the importance of achieving unity in our relationships. May we always seek to root ourselves in God's love, to build trust and intimacy in our relationships, and to reflect His glory in all that we do. And may we experience the fullness of love and life together, as we walk in faith, trust, and love, with Christ as our guide.

Chapter 15: Everlasting Love: A Promise for Eternity

Introduction

Love is a central theme of the Christian faith, a divine gift that reflects the very nature of God. Throughout Scripture, God's love is described as unfailing, unchanging, and everlasting. In Jeremiah 31:3, God declares, "I have loved you with an everlasting love; therefore I have continued my faithfulness to you." This verse captures the essence of God's eternal love—a love that transcends time, space, and circumstances. As we conclude our exploration of love in this book, it is fitting to reflect on the theme of everlasting love, connecting the promise of eternal life through Christ with the enduring nature of true love. This chapter delves into the concept of everlasting love, exploring its theological significance and its implications for our relationships, both in this life and in eternity.

The Nature of Everlasting Love

Everlasting love is a love that knows no end, a love that is eternal and unchanging. It is a love that is rooted in the very character of God, who is Himself eternal and unchanging. In a world where so much is temporary and fleeting, the concept of everlasting love offers hope, stability, and assurance. It is a love that remains steadfast, regardless of circumstances, and that promises to endure for all eternity.

1. Understanding God's Everlasting Love

The foundation of everlasting love is found in the nature of God. Scripture consistently describes God's love as eternal, unchanging, and boundless. Unlike human love, which can be fickle and conditional, God's love is steadfast and unconditional. It is a love that is not dependent on our actions or worthiness but is rooted in God's character and His commitment to His creation.

In Jeremiah 31:3, God declares, "I have loved you with an everlasting love; therefore I have continued my faithfulness to you." This verse highlights two important aspects of God's love: its eternal nature and its faithfulness. God's love is not limited by time or circumstances; it is an everlasting love that transcends all barriers. Furthermore, this love is faithful, meaning that it is consistent, reliable, and trustworthy.

God's everlasting love is also a love that is active and intentional. It is a love that seeks the well-being of His creation, that desires relationship and intimacy, and that is willing to go to great lengths to bring about redemption and restoration. This love is most clearly demonstrated in the person of Jesus Christ, who, out of love for humanity, laid down His life so that we might have eternal life.

2. The Promise of Eternal Life Through Christ

The ultimate expression of God's everlasting love is found in the promise of eternal life through Jesus Christ. Scripture teaches that through Christ's sacrificial death and resurrection, we are offered the gift of eternal life—a life that is not just a continuation of our earthly existence but a life that is marked by perfect communion with God.

In John 3:16, one of the most well-known verses in the Bible, Jesus says, "For God so loved the world that He gave His only Son, that whoever believes in Him should not perish but have eternal life." This verse encapsulates the essence of God's everlasting love—a love that is willing to give the ultimate sacrifice so that we might have the hope of eternity with Him.

The promise of eternal life is not just about life after death; it is about the quality of life that we experience here and now. Eternal life, in the biblical sense, is a life that is lived in relationship with God, a life that is characterized by love, joy, peace, and fulfillment. It is a life that begins now and continues for all eternity.

This promise of eternal life is a source of hope and assurance for believers. It reminds us that, no matter what we face in this life, we have the promise of an eternal future with God. This hope is rooted in God's everlasting love—a love that will never fail, never fade, and never end.

The Enduring Nature of True Love

While the concept of everlasting love is often associated with God's love for humanity, it also has profound implications for our human relationships. True love, as it is described in Scripture, is not just a fleeting emotion or a temporary commitment; it is an enduring, steadfast love that reflects the eternal nature of God's love.

1. True Love as a Reflection of God's Love

In the Christian understanding, true love is a reflection of God's love. Just as God's love is steadfast, faithful, and unconditional, so too is the love that we are called to show to others. This kind of love is not based on feelings or circumstances but is rooted in a commitment to the well-being of the other person.

In 1 Corinthians 13, often referred to as the "Love Chapter," the Apostle Paul describes the qualities of true love: "Love is patient, love is kind. It does not envy, it does not boast, it is not proud. It does not dishonor others, it is not self-seeking, it is not easily angered, it keeps no record of wrongs. Love does not delight in evil but rejoices with the truth. It always protects, always trusts, always hopes, always perseveres" (1 Corinthians 13:4-7).

These qualities of love reflect the enduring nature of true love. True love is patient and kind, even in the face of challenges. It is not self-seeking but is concerned with the well-being of the other person. It is a love that always protects, trusts, hopes, and perseveres—a love that endures, no matter what.

True love, as described in Scripture, is not just a human effort; it is empowered by the Holy Spirit. It is through the work of the Holy Spirit in our lives that we are able to love others with a love that reflects the enduring nature of God's love. This love is not limited by our human weaknesses or failures but is sustained by the power of God's everlasting love.

2. The Covenant of Marriage: A Reflection of Everlasting Love

One of the most profound expressions of true love in human relationships is found in the covenant of marriage. Marriage, as it is described in Scripture, is a covenant—a sacred and binding promise between a man and a woman, made before God and witnessed by others. This covenant is not just a legal or social contract; it is a reflection of God's covenant with His people, a covenant that is characterized by steadfast love, faithfulness, and commitment.

In Ephesians 5:25-33, the Apostle Paul compares the relationship between a husband and wife to the relationship between Christ and the Church. Just as Christ loved the Church and gave Himself up for her, so too are husbands called to love their wives with a self-sacrificial love. This love is not just about feelings or attraction but is a commitment to the well-being of the other person, a commitment that endures through all circumstances.

The covenant of marriage is a reflection of God's everlasting love. It is a love that is meant to endure, "for better or for worse, for richer or for poorer, in sickness and in health, until death do us part." This covenantal love is a powerful testimony to the world of the enduring nature of true love, a love that reflects the eternal love of God.

3. Love that Endures Through Trials and Challenges

True love is not immune to trials and challenges. In fact, it is often in the midst of difficulties that the enduring nature of love is most clearly seen. Trials and challenges can either strengthen a relationship or weaken it, depending on how they are navigated. True love, however, has the power to endure and even grow stronger through adversity.

In Romans 5:3-5, Paul writes, "Not only that, but we rejoice in our sufferings, knowing that suffering produces endurance, and endurance produces character, and character produces hope, and hope does not put us to shame, because God's love has been poured into our hearts through the Holy Spirit who has been given to us." This passage reminds us that trials and challenges are not just obstacles to be overcome; they are opportunities for growth and transformation.

True love is characterized by perseverance—a love that endures through difficulties, that remains steadfast in the face of trials, and that continues to hope and trust in God's faithfulness. This enduring love is a reflection of God's everlasting love, a love that never fails and never gives up.

When we face trials and challenges in our relationships, it is important to remember that we are not alone. God's everlasting love is with us, sustaining us and empowering us to love others with a love that endures. This love is not just a human effort but is rooted in the power of the Holy Spirit, who enables us to love others with a love that reflects the enduring nature of God's love.

4. The Role of Faith in Sustaining True Love

Faith plays a crucial role in sustaining true love. Faith is the foundation of our relationship with God, and it is also the foundation of our relationships with others. When our love is rooted in faith, it is sustained by the power of God's everlasting love, and it is able to endure through all circumstances.

In Hebrews 11:1, faith is described as "the assurance of things hoped for, the conviction of things not seen." This assurance and conviction are what enable us to love others with a love that endures, even when we cannot see the outcome or the future. Faith gives us the confidence to trust in God's promises and to continue loving others with a steadfast love, even in the face of challenges.

Faith also provides the strength and courage needed to persevere in love. When we face difficulties in our relationships, it is our faith in God's everlasting love that gives us the strength to continue loving, to forgive, and to seek reconciliation. This faith is not just a belief in God's love; it is a trust in His faithfulness and His ability to sustain us in our relationships.

Faith also helps us to see our relationships from an eternal perspective. When our love is rooted in faith, we are able to see beyond the temporary challenges and difficulties of this life and to focus on the eternal promise of God's love. This eternal perspective gives us the strength to persevere in love and to continue loving others with a love that reflects the enduring nature of God's love.

The Promise of Everlasting Love in Eternity

The concept of everlasting love is not just about our relationships in this life; it also points to the eternal promise of God's love in eternity. Scripture teaches that, through Christ, we are offered the gift of eternal life—a life that is marked by perfect communion with God and by the fulfillment of God's everlasting love.

1. The Fulfillment of God's Love in Eternity

The promise of everlasting love finds its ultimate fulfillment in eternity. In Revelation 21:3-4, we are given a glimpse of this eternal fulfillment: "And I heard a loud voice from the throne saying, 'Behold, the dwelling place of God is with man. He will dwell with them, and they will be His people, and God Himself will be with them as their God. He will wipe away every tear from their eyes, and death shall be no more, neither shall there be mourning, nor crying, nor pain anymore, for the former things have passed away.'"

This passage describes the culmination of God's everlasting love—a love that will be fully realized in eternity, when God's people will dwell with Him in perfect communion. In this eternal state, all the effects of sin, suffering, and death will be removed, and God's love will be fully experienced in all its fullness.

The promise of eternal life is the ultimate expression of God's everlasting love. It is a love that has no end, a love that will be experienced for all eternity in perfect communion with God. This promise gives us hope and assurance in this life, knowing that, no matter what we face, we have the promise of an eternal future with God.

2. The Role of Love in Eternal Life

Love is not just a temporary aspect of our earthly relationships; it is an eternal reality that will continue to be experienced in eternity. Scripture teaches that love is the greatest of all virtues, and it is the one that will endure forever. In 1 Corinthians 13:13, Paul writes, "So now faith, hope, and love abide, these three; but the greatest of these is love."

In eternity, our experience of love will be perfected and fulfilled in the presence of God. We will experience God's love in all its fullness, and we will also experience perfect love in our relationships with others. The divisions and barriers that exist in this life will be removed, and we will be united in perfect love with God and with one another.

This eternal reality of love gives us a glimpse of the purpose and significance of our relationships in this life. Our relationships are not just temporary or fleeting; they are a reflection of the eternal love that we will experience in eternity. This perspective gives us the motivation to love others with a love that reflects the enduring nature of God's love, knowing that our love will continue to be experienced in eternity.

3. The Hope of Reunion in Eternity

The promise of everlasting love also includes the hope of reunion in eternity. For those who have lost loved ones, the promise of eternal life offers the hope of being reunited with them in the presence of God. This hope is rooted in the assurance of God's everlasting love—a love that transcends death and that promises eternal life to all who believe in Christ.

In 1 Thessalonians 4:13-18, Paul writes to the Thessalonian believers to encourage them with the hope of the resurrection and the promise of reunion with their loved ones: "For since we believe that Jesus died and rose again, even so, through Jesus, God will bring with Him those who have fallen asleep. For this we declare to you by a word from the Lord, that we who are alive, who are left until the coming of the Lord, will not precede those who have fallen asleep. For the Lord Himself will descend from heaven with a cry of command, with the voice of an archangel, and with the sound of the trumpet of God. And the dead in Christ will rise first. Then we who are alive, who are left, will be caught up together with them in the clouds to meet the Lord in the air, and so we will always be with the Lord. Therefore encourage one another with these words."

This passage offers the hope of reunion in eternity—a hope that is grounded in the promise of God's everlasting love. It is a reminder that, for those who have put their trust in Christ, death is not the end but the beginning of an eternal life that will be marked by perfect love and communion with God and with one another.

This hope of reunion in eternity is a source of comfort and encouragement for believers. It reminds us that, no matter what we face in this life, we have the promise of an eternal future with God and with our loved ones. This hope gives us the strength to persevere in love, knowing that our love will be perfected and fulfilled in eternity.

4. Living in Light of Eternity

The promise of everlasting love and eternal life through Christ calls us to live in light of eternity. This means living with an eternal perspective, knowing that our relationships in this life are a reflection of the eternal love that we will experience in eternity. It also means living with the hope and assurance of God's everlasting love, knowing that, no matter what we face, we have the promise of an eternal future with God.

Living in light of eternity also means loving others with a love that reflects the enduring nature of God's love. This love is not just about feelings or emotions but is a commitment to the well-being of others, a commitment that endures through all circumstances. It is a love that is patient, kind, and selfless—a love that reflects the eternal love of God.

Living in light of eternity also involves living with the hope and assurance of reunion in eternity. This hope gives us the strength to persevere in love, knowing that our love will be perfected and fulfilled in eternity. It also gives us the motivation to love others with a love that reflects the enduring nature of God's love, knowing that our love will continue to be experienced in eternity.

The Transformative Power of Everlasting Love

The concept of everlasting love is not just a theological idea; it has the power to transform our lives and our relationships. When we experience and embrace God's everlasting love, it changes the way we see ourselves, the way we relate to others, and the way we live our lives.

1. The Power of Everlasting Love to Transform Our Identity

One of the most profound ways that God's everlasting love transforms our lives is by changing our identity. When we experience God's love, we are no longer defined by our past, our failures, or our weaknesses; we are defined by God's love for us. This love gives us a new identity as beloved children of God, a new purpose, and a new destiny.

In 1 John 3:1, John writes, "See what kind of love the Father has given to us, that we should be called children of God; and so we are." This verse reminds us that, because of God's love, we are given a new identity as children of God. This identity is not based on our performance or worthiness but is rooted in God's love and grace.

This new identity also gives us a new purpose and a new destiny. As children of God, we are called to live in a way that reflects God's love and to fulfill the purpose that He has for our lives. This purpose is not just about our own happiness or fulfillment but is about loving and serving others in a way that reflects the enduring nature of God's love.

2. The Power of Everlasting Love to Transform Our Relationships

God's everlasting love also has the power to transform our relationships. When we experience God's love, it changes the way we relate to others. We are no longer driven by selfishness, fear, or insecurity; we are empowered by God's love to love others with a selfless, sacrificial love.

This love transforms our relationships by creating a foundation of trust, respect, and commitment. It enables us to forgive and to seek reconciliation, even when we have been hurt. It gives us the strength to persevere in love, even in the face of challenges and difficulties. And it allows us to experience the joy and fulfillment of loving others with a love that reflects the enduring nature of God's love.

3. The Power of Everlasting Love to Transform Our Lives

Finally, God's everlasting love has the power to transform our lives. When we experience and embrace God's love, it changes the way we see ourselves, the way we relate to others, and the way we live our lives. This love gives us a new identity, a new purpose, and a new destiny. It empowers us to live with hope, assurance, and confidence, knowing that we are loved by God and that we have the promise of eternal life with Him.

This transformative power of God's love is not just about changing our behavior or our circumstances; it is about changing our hearts. It is about experiencing the fullness of God's love and allowing that love to shape and define every aspect of our lives. It is about living in light of eternity, knowing that our lives and our relationships are a reflection of the eternal love that we will experience in eternity.

Conclusion

As we conclude our exploration of love in this book, it is fitting to reflect on the theme of everlasting love—a love that transcends time, space, and circumstances, a love that is rooted in the very character of God. In Jeremiah 31:3, God declares, "I have loved you with an everlasting love; therefore I have continued my faithfulness to you." This verse captures the essence of God's eternal love—a love that remains steadfast, regardless of circumstances, and that promises to endure for all eternity.

The concept of everlasting love is not just a theological idea; it has profound implications for our lives and our relationships. It reminds us that, no matter what we face in this life, we have the promise of an eternal future with God—a future that is marked by perfect love and communion with Him. It also calls us to love others with a love that reflects the enduring nature of God's love, a love that is patient, kind, and selfless—a love that endures through all circumstances.

As we reflect on the power of God's everlasting love, let us be reminded of the importance of embracing this love in our lives and in our relationships. May we always seek to root ourselves in God's love, to love others with a love that reflects His enduring nature, and to live in light of eternity, with the hope and assurance of God's everlasting love. And may we experience the fullness of love and life together, as we walk in faith, trust, and love, with Christ as our guide.

Don't miss out!

Visit the website below and you can sign up to receive emails whenever Angela Marie Stewart publishes a new book. There's no charge and no obligation.

https://books2read.com/r/B-A-LZEHC-RCIVE

Connecting independent readers to independent writers.

Did you love *Faithful Love*? Then you should read *A Love Worth Waiting For*[1] by Angela Marie Stewart!

[2]

"A Love Worth Waiting For" explores the spiritual journey of love, offering deep theological reflections on patience, trust, purity, prayer, and more. Each chapter delves into how waiting for love reflects faith in God's timing and plan, drawing on biblical insights to inspire contentment in singleness, the joy of fulfilled love, and the ultimate fulfillment found in God's eternal love. Perfect for those seeking a Christian perspective on love and relationships, this book offers wisdom and encouragement for anyone navigating the season of waiting.

---

1. https://books2read.com/u/47wLQN

2. https://books2read.com/u/47wLQN

About the Author

Angela Marie Stewart is a cherished author known for her heartfelt Christian romance fiction. With a passion for weaving tales that inspire faith and love, Angela's novels explore the transformative power of grace and the enduring strength of the human spirit. Her writing journey reflects her deep commitment to portraying love stories grounded in Christian values and spiritual growth. Angela's work resonates with readers seeking uplifting narratives and the comfort of faith intertwined with romance. When she's not writing, Angela enjoys community service, spending time with her family, and exploring the beauty of her surroundings.